# RAISINS IN MILK

*To Ganga,
a fountain of memories*

Library of Congress Cataloguing in publication data.

Covin, David 1940 -
Raisins in Milk

1. Coming of Age in Florida - 2. Black girl - 3. 1913 -1920
- 4. Fiction.

I. Title

ISBN- 13: 978-0-9844350-7-4

Published by Blue Nile Press, 2018

Cover Art by Claire Jacobson

Cover Design by Dinah Yisrael

Manufactured in the United States of America

## Also by David Covin

*Prodigal* (a novel)

*Princes of the Road* (a novel)

*Wimbey's Corner* (a novel)

*Black Politics After the Civil Rights Movement:
Activity and Beliefs in Sacramento, 1970 - 2000*

*The Unified Black Movement in Brazil, 1978 - 2002*

*The African Race in California, Darkness Visible*

*Brown Sky* (a novel)

In 1977, when Toni Morrison was an editor for Random House, she read an early version of *Raisins in Milk*. In a letter she wrote to the author, she said "... I loved so much of the writing .... The prose, the description that is the omnipresent omniscient author's, is splendid." But the woman who would go on to win the Nobel Prize for literature also said, "The real problem ... is that the characters seem thinner and more conventional than they are."

The author has spent the intervening years revising the story, addressing Ms. Morrison's concerns. The central question is whether he has met the challenge offered forty years ago by the country's foremost writer. That will be for the reader to decide. This can definitely be said. From the first page of *Raisins in Milk* the reader enters an unknown world. No living human being has a personal memory of Jacksonville, Florida in 1900. Yet that time and place had an eradicable impact on life in the United States that continues today, one hundred and eighteen years later. Once you turn the first page and enter the world of Ruth-Ann Weathering, you will understand why.

*Was running through the fields one day*
*Sis Avery's chopping corn*
*Big horse come stomping after me*
*I knowed then I was gone*

*Sis Avery grabbed that horse's mane*
*And not one minute late*
*Cause trembling down behind her*
*I seen my ugly fate*

*She hollered to that horse to "Whoa!*
*I gotcha hoppy-toad."*
*And yonder came the goopher man*
*A-running down the road.*

From Margaret Walker, "Ballad of the Hoppy Toad."

*Mandarin, Florida*

*Springtime* 1913

# 1

The breeze that came in from the sea was warm. It brought with it also the smell of the sea. It blew across the broad reach of the warm, clear river, like an arm of the sea itself, so wide it was. A sparkle in the air foretold a day of deep blue sky. Dawn held a darkening, the sun still below the eastern horizon.

The horse in the middle of an immense field measured eighteen hands. His head up, ears alert, black, he posed gleaming and still, the moving air lifting the hairs on his tail and rustling his long mane.

Tall, lush grass, large trees, flush with the foliage of early summer spread over the vast enclosure, bound on all four sides by solid oak posts, eight feet tall. Four rows of beams spanned each post. A heavy and vicious barbed wire topped the beams and encircled the posts. Three strong men were required to open the massive gate, locked and secured by strong chains. For a mile, one side of the fence ran next to a drainage ditch, separating it from the brown, arrow-straight, dirt road. Ruth-Ann strode rapidly, her bare toes making marks in the lane's moist surface. Her belt, looped to hold her lunch, books, paper, and pencil, swung from her right hand.

Her younger siblings were not with her. Of all the pupils in the school, she alone took the walk this morning. Five years had passed since a child had finished the eighth grade. Now, it was about to happen again. Ruth-Ann laughed with joy and excitement.

She was getting two extra days of school to prepare her graduation speech.

The sun broke free from the horizon, burning red and orange. The sky purpled, shading to darkest blue. Ruth-Ann inhaled the cool air. She moved fluidly, erect like a dancer, her head high. The light caught, full, her broad cheekbones, the color of bright honey. Thick, black hair hung down her back in four braids. Average height, she appeared tall. Her strong frame carried her ample figure with grace.

Deep in the field, almost out of sight from the road, shielded by scattered trees, the stallion held motionless. Almost imperceptibly, life seemed to infuse him. His ears twitched and pointed forward. He tilted his head back, raising his muzzle. He lifted the skin of his mouth from his teeth. He dropped his head, shaking his neck. Fully animated, he snorted, and raising his hooves high in the air, pranced in a circle. Then, smoothly, beautifully, he trotted towards the fence, towards the road.

Ruth-Ann saw him coming, saw him roll his wild eye up into his head, the white gleaming malevolently, saw him break into a gallop straight at her.

She stopped. Before her eyes he grew, blotting out the bright sun. Her mind clicked. *Run, Run!*

Her face stretched into a mask of terror, she began to run away from her home, in the direction of the school. The package swung wildly at the end of the strap in her hand.

The girl's movement changed the horse's angle. His great strides sent him striking over the earth, sending clods of dirt and grass into the air.

Ruth-Ann started at a sprint but shifted down to a pace she could maintain until she reached the end of the demon's fence. She

2

didn't look back. She ran.

Suddenly he was beside her. She felt the heat from him, felt the ground shaking, heard his horrible sounds. She heard the splitting, the cracking, as his heavy body crashed into the fence. She heard his mad whinny of pain and rage. She ran.

Blood streaming from where the heavy beams had cut his skin, the horse glanced off the fence, circled into a loop, and attacked it, raising up on his powerful hind legs, raking his hooves at the redoubtable structure.

The girl ran on. She felt a hand squeezing her heart, but she drove her legs on, flailing at the air with her belt and its package. She heard the horse screaming. She heard the thuds against the heavy wood. She did not see anything.

The horse, streaked with blood and flecked with foam, launched himself at the fence again and again. He knew where it ended. He tore great holes in the ground with his charges. He knew where the escape point was for his target. He wanted to be through the barrier and onto her before she reached it.

The girl could not hear herself, could not hear her painful gasps for air, could not feel the tears streaming down her cheeks, hardly felt the woodenness of her limbs, the lunch and books bumping over the ground.

Then - the fence was gone. She ran on struggling, stumbling. At last, the world before her opened up. The bizarre, chilling screams and sounds of tortured wood were behind her - receding. The feeling of freedom buoyed her and she ran faster. Until she found herself on her knees, the grass wet with dew, coarse against her skin, trying, trying with all her might, to breathe. She choked, gasped - sobbed, drew air into her lungs, desperately. Her aching, trembling body collapsed on the serrated, damp grass.

3

Breathing hurt. Breathing hurt. She closed her eyes. "Thank you, Jesus," she said. "Thank you, Jesus."

She looked down the road. She couldn't see the fence. Nothing. She rested awhile. She looked behind her. Nothing. Slowly, she got to her feet. She was alright. Her breath was coming back. She could walk, still trembling, but she could walk. *Thank you, Jesus.* One step at a time. Her knees wanted to give way. One step at a time. Her lungs ached. One step at a time. Look back down the road. Nothing. One step at a time. Her clothes stuck to her. One step at a time.

Far behind her, the black stallion, his skin torn, smeared with blood and sweat, faced his nemesis - the fence. He charged it again and again, throwing his full weight against it, to no avail. He succeeded only in inflicting more wounds upon himself. Then, in a desperate fury, he turned and fired out against a post with both back hooves. Contact! Once, twice, three times he launched his full hatred against the post through his powerful hind legs. With a resounding "crack" the solid post broke at its base and tumbled over, carrying cross beams and barbed wire with it.

The triumphant horse wheeled, sailed over the downed obstacle, and gained the road. Once on the dirt surface, he shook his magnificent neck and head. He seemed to float as he cantered down the way, his mane and tail teased by the breeze.

## 2

Gradually, a steadiness returned to Ruth-Ann's stride. The sun and the beauty of the day filtered into her spirit, into her body. It was broad daylight, she realized, not darkest night. The sky was bright. She had escaped. She resisted the impulse to look over her shoulder again. If she didn't see him, he wasn't there. Slowly, she began to calm down, to look around her, to re-engage herself with the world.

Birds twittered and trilled in the trees and high grasses. Frogs croaked from the drainage ditch. The air felt soft, warm and moist. The scent of the world's waters filled her nostrils. She began to regain a bit of lilt to her step. Glancing down, she saw the dangling little bundle, the strap still wrapped around her hand, the package intact. She smiled.

\*

The sound, like a staccato drum-beat - an instant of nothing - then sound again, struck her with a feeling of unreality. She felt her insides turning. She kept walking, eyes straight ahead, hoping not to hear the sound again, hoping it was an accident, some trick played by the wind. But the hard, swift, separated sounds, did not stop.

They came on. Clearer now. Louder. She did not want to acknowledge them. She did not want to give them substance. She walked, refusing to believe, refusing to look over her shoulder. She was conscious of each step. Each silent footfall. Because behind her was not silence. Behind her was sound. She took one step at a time but she was no longer aware of what she did. Her whole reality had become sound.

Louder.

Sound.

Her refusal to believe did not make the sounds go away.

She stopped. She closed her eyes.

*Dear God, I put myself in your hands.*

She opened her eyes.

She turned her head slowly, looking back over her right shoulder. What she could see of the road was empty, but 100 yards behind her the road curved around a dense stand of trees. What was behind the trees she could not see. She turned her head to face forward again and picked up her pace. She looked over her shoulder again. Nothing. She kept looking. Nothing.

Then, black and flowing, mane in the air, he rounded the corner.

She could not will herself to move. She could not even turn her head back around. The horse consumed her sight. Her feet sank roots into the earth. Her package had become a leaden ball chaining her to the ground. Her legs had become carven pillars. In her mouth she felt the beating of her heart.

She stood motionless watching death descend upon her.

"Ruth-Ann!"

The shout spun her around, shocked her into sensibility. She tried to step forward as her head whirled, but tripped, stumbled, fell, on her back, into the ditch.

The warm water smacked into her shoulder blades and the back of her head. She felt wetness engulfing her, saw grasses

6

bending over the opening of the ditch above her.

Almost immediately the narrow strip of sky filled with the demonic stallion. Rearing above her, seeming to reach the blue arch of the heavens, the black beast raised his fore hoofs in the air and screamed. Next he was coming down, down, his hooves like sharpened bludgeons - flashing. They tore up the ground around the top of the ditch. Clods of dirt and stalks of grass tumbled down onto Ruth-Ann. Yet the horse refused to let his feet down into the cavity. He reared and came down and thrashed above Ruth-Ann, but his hooves would not descend into the opening.

She stared - afraid to hope, afraid to think, unable to move. Except for her face, her whole head and body were covered by warm water. Fury raged above her. The voice, contrapuntal against the crazed blaring of the horse, blasted into her brain.

"Git! Git! Git!, you black devil! Git on outa heah!"

Mr. Harris. His voice. Yes, it was him. He lived with Mrs. Harris and their boys, not far from where she must be. *Mr. Harris!*

"Git! Git, I said! Git - Hyah! Hyah!"

Suddenly Ruth-Ann was looking past the torn edges of the cavity to blue sky.

The horse was screaming and she could hear its hooves.

"Hyah! Hyah! Git! Outah heah! Git! Hyah!"

She sat up. She felt the water welding her dress to her. She went to her knees, her hands grasped the edge of the trench. The dirt under her wet fingers turned to mud. She peered out of her refuge.

The huge horse and Mr. Harris seemed in the midst of a grotesque dance. The horse pranced, his neck arched, then reared, hooves slicing the air. He came down, circling Mr. Harris, moving in and out, screaming. Mr. Harris whirled a gigantic axe about himself, the blade flashing in the sun. The axe tore through the air, making a whipping, rhythmic sound. Mr. Harris stepped forward, then, back, always facing the horse. His voice rang.

"Git! Hyah! Outah heah!"

The horse stopped. It backed up. It turned and cantered a short distance. It spun around and faced Mr. Harris. It stood still.

Mr. Harris let the axe blade fall to the ground. Leaning on the handle he glanced in Ruth-Ann's direction.

His eye caught her head poised above the ditch.

"Ruth-Ann, git ovuh to the house! Run! Now!"

She climbed out of the depression, her right hand holding to the strap still wrapped around it. She saw the Harris house sitting in the middle of the field across the road. Mrs. Harris stood on the porch. Ruth-Ann started to run.

That set off the horse. He dashed to get around Mr. Harris. But the man and his whirling axe were too quick. The horse turned, went the other way. The man was there, blocking him again. The girl ran automatically, not feeling her legs. She was on the porch, in Mrs. Harris' arms. Mrs. Harris held her closely.

"Let's get on in, Ruth-Ann. We'll leave the door open behind us." Mrs. Harris backed into the door, holding Ruth-Ann.

Out in the field, the horse concentrated his attention on Mr. Harris. Their dance had resumed. This time, Mr. Harris was inching it slowly, slowly, towards the house.

The horse wheeled away from Mr. Harris again. When it turned around and stopped, Mr. Harris was not where he had been. Holding the axe close to the blade, he had broken into a dash and was twenty yards from the porch.

The stallion charged after him, its whinny a horror of sound.

Mr. Harris hit one step, then the porch. Mrs. Harris slammed the door behind him. Like an echo the crazed animal banged onto

8

the steps, crashed onto the porch and rammed into the walls of the house. For two or three minutes the horse stomped on the porch, kicked out boards in the house's wall. Then, one of his hooves went through a board in the porch floor. Yanking it out, he soared off the porch and galloped away.

Inside, the three people who had pushed the table against the door, stood staring at the door, breathing heavily.

They looked through a window. The horse was disappearing from view.

Ruth-Ann was first to speak. "Oh, thank you. Thank you. I'm so sorry. Thank you, Mr. Harris and Mrs. Harris. Thank you. Thank you. I'm so sorry. I didn't mean t'do this to you. I'm so sorry."

"Hush up, girl," said Mrs. Harris, putting her arms around Ruth-Ann and pulling her close. "We just glad we was heah. Just glad we could do somethin`."

"Yes'm," said Ruth-Ann, holding tightly to Mrs. Harris. She started shaking as she cried, "Thank you, thank you, so much. Oh, Mrs. Harris, thank you, so much."

Mr. Harris walked the axe over to the corner by the stove.

"Yes, indeedy," he said. "We was watchin` you walk down the road. Sech a fine figure of a young woman you's done growed up t` be."

"Mr. Harris - you," Ruth-Ann raised her tear-coursed face from Mrs. Harris' shoulder to look at her family's long-time friend. "I -"

"Don't you mind, Ruth-Ann," he said. "We was watchin` you and talkin` 'bout how we used t'see you an` yo` Daddy down at the St. Johns diggin` clams when you wasn't nothin` but a little bitty thing. You `member that?"

9

"Yes sir."

"You was the cutest thing - diggin` clams. Ha! Nevuh will fogit it.

"That's what we was talkin` about. Then - then, Martha said look'd like somethin` was wrong with you. I'd - I'd went ovuh to the stove ... was standin` theah. Then, she said - 'Oh, my Lord, my sweet Lord!' I heard it in her voice. I just grabbed the axe and run out the do`. I seen him. Seen you. Started runnin`. Called yo` name."

Ruth-Ann sobbed. She could only say, "Thank you. Thank you." She kept repeating it through her weeping.

Mr. Harris walked over and patted his wife and Ruth-Ann on their shoulders. He pushed the table away from the door. "I'm gon` go find the boys," he said. "We gon` go tell Mr. Cooper t'roun` up his devil-hoss and keep him penned in befo` somebody kill him." He walked out of the door, surveyed the damage on the porch, then jumped down and strode away.

"You got a good husband, Mrs. Harris," said Ruth-Ann.

"Yes. He's alright," said Mrs. Harris. "He's alright for a old man." She laughed. "Come on girl. You looks a mess."

# 3

Ruth-Ann told Mrs. Harris she had only two more days before she would graduate and that she had to make a speech. Mrs. Harris said, yes, she knew. The whole family planned to attend the graduation. It had been so long since they'd had one. They were all right proud of Ruth-Ann. Ruth-Ann cleaned up. Together, the two of them washed her blouse, skirt, and under things. Ruth-Ann made the fire in the stove to heat the iron, and they took turns ironing her clothes as they talked. When they finished, the clothes were both dry and pressed. Ruth-Ann went on to school. Mrs. Harris watched her down the road until she was out of sight.

\*

Mr. Turner talked Ruth-Ann into letting him walk her home. A mile before they reached the Harrises', Ruth-Ann's father, Emanuel, met them on the road. He had learned of the attack and was on his way to the school to meet Ruth-Ann. He invited Mr. Turner to come home with them for supper. Mr. Turner accepted.

On the way, Emmanuel Weathering told them what he had heard of the happenings after the devil horse had galloped away from the Harrises'.

"Yassuh," he said. "John Harris run down them boys o' his'n. Found 'em at the St. Johns. The three of 'em walked ovuh t' Coopuh's. Ain't seen the hoss. Hoss done gone.

11

"John Harris, he walked right up t' Coopuh's front do` - may God strak me ef Ah'm lyin`. Right up t'Coopuh's front do` - him an` them two big boys o` his'n. Beat on the do`.

"Chahlie opened the do` - you know - Chahlie Stukes. He work theah. Chahlie opened the do`. Ha, ha, ha, ha! Ol' Chahlie. He liked t`had a fit!

"He say," Emanuel broke into laughter. Recovering himself, he said, "He say - you know - he whisper like. He say ..." Emanuel imitated Charlie's small, tight voice going into a whisper.

"'Y'all, cain't come t`the front do! What's wrong with y'all! G'on `roun` t` the back! G'on!'

"An` he slam the do` on 'em.

"John, he jest beat on the do` agin. Yes, he did! Ah ain't lyin`! Beat on it agin. Yelled out, 'Is Mr. Robut Coopuh in heah!' With God as my witness.

"Well, Chahlie, he jest snatched that do` open. Done toined culluh by now. 'Culluds goes to th`back do`,' he say.

"'Ah'll go t`any damn do` jest long's Ah sees Mr. Robut Coopuh,' says John. Didn't he!

"Bout that time Mr. Robut Coopuh standin` right in the do'.

"'What this mean,' he say.

"John tol` him he ain't had time fo no nigga mannas. Said, 'Mr. Coopuh. You got a big ol` black hoss nama Nightmare. `Les you 'roun` up some boys an` catch that devil. You gon` find him laid open. He broke down his fence. Chased Emanuel Weatherin's girl down by my place. Damn neah killed her. If he ain't put up good `n tight by this evenin`, me and my boys heah, we gon` run him down an` kill him.'

"That was three big mens stan`in` theah lookin' at Mr. Coopuh. Three *big* mens.

12

"'Kin you hep,' say Mr. Coopuh.
"'We's heah,' say John.
"Mr. Coopuh say, "Tha's all Ah wants t'know.'"

Mr. Weathering told how Mr. Cooper had walked right by a stupefied Charlie, how the four men had rounded up five of Mr. Cooper's hands and some horses. They went down to the Dawson's where they got the Dawson boys and three hands. Eventually, there were sixteen men and eight horses out looking for Nightmare.

They spotted him in the swamp country, right where Mill Creek splits up into sloughs. Then it took all of them almost the whole day to catch him. He kept them going along the meadows and forests that edged the swamp, sprinting ahead, doubling back when they tried to head him off. There was no question about it, he was not only mean, he was smart. Eventually, they hemmed him in, got him roped and hobbled.

The Harrises had told Mr. Weathering that the horse was going to be kept chained and hobbled, and that his fence was going to be re-enforced. It was quite an adventure, one which his eldest daughter had sparked off, and it had a happy ending. Emanuel glimmered as he told the tale.

13

**4**

Jason and Wilma tore down the road toward the approaching trio, their little arms and legs churning through clouds of dust. Their high voices carried in the evening stillness.

"Ah'm gon` beat you, you little burr-head!"

"No you ain't, you snot-nose pickaninny!"

"Ruth-Ann! Ruth Ann!"

"We heard! We heard!"

They had not recognized Mr. Turner.

"Daddy! Daddy!"

They did not look up again, intent upon their race, until they were on top of the incoming walkers.

"I beat!"

"*I* beat!"

"No, you -"

"Mr. Turner!"

"Mr. Turner!"

In unison, "Good afternoon, Mr. Turner."

They were suddenly sweetness and light. Angelic smiles shone from their small, panting faces.

Mr. Weathering dropped a large hand on each of their shoulders.

"Well, Jason and Wilma," he said, "what did you heah?"

Excitement immediately agitated the two children. They turned their attention to Ruth-Ann.

"We heard," said Wilma, fastening her eyes on her big sister, "'bout Ruth-Ann and Nightmare!"

"Yeah," chimed in Jason.

"Did it really happen, Ruth-Ann," asked Wilma.

"Did it," echoed Jason.

Ruth-Ann smiled. She did not know how to start, though she had been thinking about what she would say all day long. She just kept smiling.

"Ruth-Ann!"

"They said," went on Wilma, suddenly no longer able to keep waiting for an answer, "that Nightmare chased you all the way from his field to down by the Harrises', said he knocked you in the ditch, said -"

"Ruth-Ann," cried Jason, "Your dress ain't even dirty! You ain't been in no ditch!"

"Haven't been in any ditch," corrected Ruth-Ann.

"Oh, yes, I'm sorry, Mr. Turner. Haven't been in any ditch. Ruth-Ann - you haven't been in any ditch. Look how clean you are!"

"Daddy, Mr. Turner," Ruth-Ann smiled, "I must say I think Jason is disappointed. He wanted me to have a hole in my head and my teeth knocked out. He wanted me to be all covered with blood, with great rips in my dress."

Jason's eyes widened and he almost nodded his head, yes.

"I'm sorry to disappoint you," she said, hugging Jason and kissing him on his cheek, "but Nightmare has never been fast enough to get that close to me."

Wilma's eyes widened this time. "You mean you outran

15

Nightmare?"

"All I know is," said Ruth-Ann as she began to saunter closer to the house, "my dress isn't torn or messy, I don't have a scratch on me." She twirled the strap dangling from her hand, "and all my possessions are in good condition."

Mr. Weathering looked at Mr. Turner. "Who would a` guessed it? Ah've raised me a whole family full o` Br'er Rabbits?"

"Sakes alive," said Jason. "What did happen, Ruth-Ann, huh? What did happen? We thought you'd be all wet and messy from the ditch - sakes alive, what did happen?"

Ruth-Ann walked on in silence, a study in nonchalance, swinging her hips from one side of the road to the other, an air of mystery about her.

Wilma and Jason followed her, subdued, mute, entranced.

Mr. Weathering and Mr. Turner, chuckling to each other, walked behind the two smaller children, unable to keep their eyes off the unfolding comedy.

*

The topic of conversation at supper that evening was predictable and irrepressible.

Daphne, who was next to Ruth-Ann in age, said, "They say the reason Mr. Harris got out to the road so fast is that they could hear Ruth-Ann hollerin' a mile away."

"That's right," said Paul, who was not quite a year younger than Daphne, "but Ruth-Ann was runnin` so fast, that by the time he got outside, she had already passed by his house."

Everybody laughed.

16

"Mm, mm, mm," chuckled Mrs. Weathering. "If she's that fast, Ah wondas what take her so long t' fix breakfus?"

"Or iron clothes," threw in Daphne.

"Or hoe the garden," joined Paul.

"Or -" piped up Wilma.

"You be quiet," said Ruth-Ann. Don't you or Jason open your mouths. Y'all too little to even *think* about makin' fun o' me. And come to think about it, too ugly, too."

Laughing, Mr. Turner said, "Mrs. Weathering, could you pass me those biscuits, please?

"You know, Mrs. Weathering, bein' a bachelor, I don't get a chance to eat this way very much, and your cooking is just delicious."

"Oh, thank you, Mr. Turner," she answered. "It's a honor to me. An ah jest loves t'see a hongry man eat. So don't stop till you jest cain't lift yo' hand no mo'.

"You know, when the school fust started out, schoolmaster use t' eat at a diffrunt fam'ly's house every night. Changed that I guess, now that the school bode pay the teacher."

"Yes, Mrs. Weathering," said Mr. Turner. "I guess that's the reason." For an instant the joy left his face. "But this is better," he continued, "than all the pay envelopes in the state of Florida." He took a bite of biscuit.

"My, my, my," said Mr. Weathering. "Y'all gon' let our hongry guest - no offense, Mr. Turner - make us fogit about ouha little hero." He patted Ruth-Ann on her forearm. "Yes, we got us a real little hero."

Ruth-Ann swallowed the food in her mouth and smiled.

"Yes, indeedy," said Mr. Weathering. "But y'all been underestimatin' Nightmare. Tha's one fast hoss, an' as fast as Ah

17

believes Ruth-Ann done run, ah don't believe she could out run him. No. That hoss too fast. No, John Harris tol` me the real reason ol' Nightmare ain't caught Ruth-Ann." His eyes twinkled. His family became quiet and tried to keep the smiles off their faces as they held their eyes down on their plates.

"He say when he come outside his do`, he seen Ruth-Ann flyin` down the road, Nightmare one step behin` her, gainin` on her, `bout t` ketch her. Say Ruth-Ann looked back ovuh huh shoulda an` seen that hoss jest about t` knock huh down. Say Ruth-Ann was so scairt," he paused. He drew it out as long as he could, "so scairt ... she turnt white! Tha`s right. Turnt white! Well. Nightmare, he stopped dead in the road. He knowed he wasn't supposed t` be chasin` no white woman! Jest stopp't still, an` shook his head. Tha`s how ouha little hero got away from the devil hoss - she turnt white!"

The whole group erupted in merriment.

"Well, take it from yo` Mama, Ruth-Ann," said Mrs. Weathering, "if you could pull that trick ev'y time you got in trouble, you'd save yosef a whole lot o` grief in this life."

Everyone in the room, mouths loaded with food, nodded vigorously.

"I know one thing," said Ruth-Ann, looking intentionally from each of her brothers and sisters to the next, trying to recoup some of the glory the day's excitement had heaped upon her, "I won't have to walk that road everyday *next* year."

Ruth-Ann, her parents, and Mr. Turner opened up laughing at four dropped little faces.

Later on, they would each, one by one, get Ruth-Ann's story, her full, true story of what had happened. But not this night. This night it was too new, too exciting, too big. It would have to remain mythical and undefined, an occasion for wild extravagances and craziness - too real to try to touch.

In the twilight, the younger children played in the field across the road, invisible, but audible. Occasionally, the flash of a shirt or a pair of pants caught the eye. But mostly laughs and shrieks and shouts marked their presence.

Inside, Ruth-Ann and her mother washed the dishes. Mrs. Weathering kept a monologue going about her pride over the graduation. Ruth-Ann monitored her mother's words, but she did not listen. Her ear was trying to pick up what the two men outside were saying. There was a certain earnestness in their tone.

"I wish it weren't true, Mr. Weathering," Mr. Turner said, "But I'm afraid this will be the last time I ever walk this road back to the school."

"The young-uns is gon` miss you, Mr. Turner. An` they ain't th` only ones. Heps us. Heps all of us t` have a young man like you `roun`.

"Ah. Ah don't thank you knows how good it is, t` have somebody, t` have one of us `roun` what we kin look up to. Somebody what's got hissef a education. Somebody kin read an` write with the best of `em. Somebody. A young man what won't be breakin` his back all his life so's his chirrens kin eat, an` his wife kin have one good dress, an` so some no-good white man kin git fattuh and richuh. Somebody ... somebody who ... we kin say, we can say to ouha chirrens. This is yo` future. Not me. Not yo` mama, but this young man. This heah is yo` future.

"You know," said Mr. Weathering, "we was special to ouha folks - the missuz and me - when we was chirrens. We was the future to them. They tol` us all the time. Because, you see, we *was* special. We *was* diffrunt. We hadn't lived up under no slavery. We

19

was *diffrunt*. We wasn't borned up under it. We ain't never lived up under it. Ouha Mamas and Papas ain't never seen no Colored folks like us. We ain't never been no slaves. So they kept on tellin` us how we was diffrunt. How we was the future.

"Now, I don't know what slavery were like, `ceptin` what I done heard people say. An` it sound bad t` me, it sound terrible bad. But all I really knows is if it were worser than this heah, then it got t` be somethin` I don't see how nobody lived through it. Because this heah, ... what Mrs. Weatherin` an` me done been through ... I wouldn't wish it on a dog.

"So I knows. I knows we ain't lived through what ouha folks done lived through. Praise God. Ouha lives was bettuh than theahs. But it ain't no good life. Matter of fact, it's a bad life. A hard life. So when I wants Ruth-Ann an` them t`think on the future, I don't want `em thinkin` `bout a life like ouhas. I don't want `em thinkin` `bout us. I wants `em thinkin` `bout a bettuh life. I wants `em thinkin` `bout somebody like you."

For a few moments they sat in silence. Ruth-Ann strained to hear while she dutifully grunted and chuckled in response to her mother's observations and anecdotes.

"I felt that, Mr. Weathering," Mr. Turner said. "I felt that, too. And I felt ... I felt I should really try to be some kind of example ... someone ... it was worthwhile to look up to - someone - it was worthwhile saying to your children, 'This is the future. It is a good future. It is a proud future.'

"Yes, you see ... I felt this very much.

"And so. And so, I thought I should try to be ... an example. I ... I ... last month .... Last month I went down to the registrar's office to register to vote."

"Oh, my God."

20

"I know. But I felt I should. I ... believed ... I should. If I am the future. And if the future is to mean anything, then we must act like men. We cannot. We cannot sit in the shadows. I mean. I really do believe we must act like men. Not beasts, do you understand? Not beasts!

"So. They were polite. They said, 'Oh, you're the school teacher over there by Stowe's aren't you?'

"I said, 'Yessir.'

"They said. 'Well, it's nice to see your better class of coloreds.' And they let me fill out the application.

"But last week, Tuesday, Mr. Hunt, he's the president of the school committee. Mr. Hunt had me into his office. He said. He said.

"'Nathaniel, the school will not be requiring your services past the end of this term.'

"I said, 'Is it because I registered?'

"He said, 'We don't need no niggas in this county think they big enough to vote.' And I'm using his own words, excuse me, Mr. Weathering, but he said, 'and especially not no god-damn darky school teacher think's he's bigger than his coon britches anyway. That what you teachin` them pickaninnies? To vote! `Fore you know it, we'll have every burr-head in the county trying to act like a goddamned white man - worse than reconstruction!'"

"They ain't human," said Mr. Weathering. "Ah sweahs they ain't human, an` they don't know the love o` God. They's the meanest, lowest thang on this God's earth."

"He told me, he told me that when I finished this term, I would get my last pay envelope, and he didn't want to see me anywhere near Jacksonville. Said it'd probably be best if I got out of Florida, got out of the South altogether because I didn't know how

21

to act. Said I'd be better off in the North somewhere, where they could afford to play with fancy niggers like me."

"Well, Mr. Turner, maybe he's right about one thing?"

"What's that?"

"That it's better jest t` go an` git on up out `n the South. Cause this ain't no wheah fo` a man t` live. Least ways not a Colored man."

"Maybe. I don't know. But ... he made it clear, he made it clear that if I didn't get out, least away from Jacksonville, they'd know where to find me."

"Devils. I sweah, Mr. Turner, the white man is a devil."

"Anyway, Mr. Weathering, I'm gonna be leaving as soon as the term is over. I haven't told anyone else yet. But just being out here with you and your family this evening, and the good food, and the fellowship, and the laughter, and ... knowing ... knowing it would be the last time, I thought I'd tell you. But I'd appreciate it, if you didn't tell anyone else. I haven't, and I haven't decided when or how I'm going to do it."

"Yessuh. You got mah word. An` mah word is mah bond. But what you gon` do? Wheah you gon` go?"

"I don't know. I been thinkin` about goin` to Hampton or Tuskeegee. Get some more schoolin`. But I don't know. I've saved some, but I'll still have to find work."

"Well, whatevuh you do, son, you got mah blessins. An` if y`evuh thank we kin hep. If you evuh gits in a tight spot, an` could use a dollah or two. Sen` for it. You heah me, sen` fo' it!"

"Every Negro in this county will do whatevuh he can t` hep you, son. You ought t` know that. When you gets ready t`let folks know `bout yo` plans, let me know. The people deserves the chance to show you how they feels. We'll get t` gethuh and raise a little somethin` fo` you. So gettin` that extry schoolin` won't be quite so hard as you's thinkin` it might be. Because, son, when you does this, you might not would know it, but you ain't jest doin` it fo` yosef. You doin` it fo` all of us, an`fo` ouha chirrens. So, I wants t` make sure that you gives us the chance t` show how much we appreciates what you wants t` do, an` what you done already did fo` all of us. We needs a chance, Mr. Turner, to tell you, Thank you."

"Yessir. Thank you. I feel mighty blessed in that. I will."

There was silence again. Deep inside her, Ruth-Ann felt something tearing.

"Mr. Weathering," Mr. Turner's voice was even more subdued.

Ruth-Ann tensed her whole being to capture his words.

"There's one other thing I should say to you. It's about Ruth-Ann."

She felt as if someone had slapped her face. For an instant she could not breathe. Then, swiftly, very swiftly, she felt herself burning.

He was going on, "Ruth-Ann ... is very smart. She is an intelligent girl ... and I mean ... well, Ruth-Ann, I'm sure you know she's a quick study. But it's more than that. She goes deep. She .... There are not many people like her. Let me, let me tell you something. I ... I finished the tenth grade. Ruth-Ann is just now finishing the eighth. But she knows more, she knows more than I do about literature, and science, and philosophy, and mathematics. She's gone past what I could teach her. For a year I've been having her do extra work that's more than I can teach her. She's been teaching herself. She is an unusual girl with unusual gifts.

"Mr. Weathering, if there's any way you can do it, I would recommend that you get her  to the Colored high school in

23

Jacksonville. I know she doesn't want to go. I know she wants to stop school now - she thinks she's a woman. And I know it would be hard for the family to keep her in school - moneywise. But if there is any way, if there is any way, please do it. Our people need Ruth-Ann. We need people with her abilities. You told me how I represent the future. Well. Ruth-Ann is the best of what the future can be. If we give her the chance - we can help build - for our people - a world that your folks and my folks - that you and I - never dreamed of. When we, as a people, find somebody like Ruth-Ann, we ought to get behind her and help her to go as far as she can. Don't let her waste away cooking grits in somebody's kitchen - I know she wants to be a cook. Or don't let her go sharecroppin` with some young buck and dropping babies till her back and her spirit break. You've got a girl there who's been blessed, Mr. Weathering. Don't let her forsake her gifts. If she finished high school, she could maybe go on to college. There's no telling what a girl with her talent can do."

Ruth-Ann's head spun. She could not listen any more. She excused herself from her mother and went out the back door. In the evening stillness she stood with her bare feet on the damp ground. All the noises of the world whirled through her head. Her body hurt.

She was still standing, leaning against the house, when Mr. Turner walked away down the road, and later on when the noises across the road had stopped, had been transformed into smaller sounds inside the house. It was only when she pushed herself away from the house and began to walk off into the darkness that the movement freshened her senses, brought the bouquet of the river to her nostrils and reminded her that in the Year of Our Lord, 1913, she was but thirteen years old, was about to be graduated from the eighth grade, and had her whole life before her.

24

# 5

Ruth-Ann stood up behind the podium. Mr. Turner had fashioned its deep-wood shining surfaces with his own hands. She looked over the people facing her. She knew each one, each face. They were all scrubbed clean and wearing their best clothes. Almost all the children had been lightly massaged with some kind of grease to keep down the ash. They glowed with the sheen. Everyone was excited, excited and stiff, scared because they were wearing their best clothes for a special occasion.

Ruth-Ann caught the twinkling eyes of several children who had shared the schoolhouse with her. They were, with great effort, exerting themselves not to squirm, helped along by friendly pressure from their parents' restraining hands.

Daphne, Paul, Wilma, and Jason sat next to Mama and Papa, very still. They waited nervously. They were a little afraid of their big sister's making a speech. They were a little annoyed at the minimal stir which continued throughout the room. They thought everyone should be as attentive and as impressed as they were. Almost everyone was. At least a dozen of those present were Weathering cousins. It was a big occasion.

Rachel and Emanuel Weathering were the proudest people in the room, though everyone was proud. Ruth-Ann was their own, a child grown up among them, helped by all of them. She stood, one who had learned to read, as many of the adults could not. She spoke the King's own English. This they all knew. More than one pair of eyes dropped tears down dark cheeks.

Ruth-Ann sought out specific faces for reassurance. Mr. and Mrs. Harris sat quietly, beaming proudly, their giant sons, Calter and Bodell, sitting next to them. Wanda Huddle, who was Ruth-Ann's own age, smiled her big, shy smile at Ruth-Ann and dropped her eyes, nervously playing with something in her hands.

Mr. Turner rose and moved to the front of the podium, slightly to the right of it. The assemblage hushed.

"I am proud this evening," he began.

As he talked, Ruth-Ann looked at the people.

Gaspry Jones, he is a cute boy, she thought. Sharecropping with his brothers over to the Duval's since he left school. Cute boy - too bad he's so silly with no get-up. I could have been very fond of old Gaspry Jones. She smiled at him. He smiled back. She could see Reuben Hawkins trying to catch her eye, winking and nodding. She let her gaze slide right by him as if she didn't see. She laughed to herself. Serves him right, she thought. Smart-behind boy.

Oh, Granny-Mame! Ruth's heart jumped with excitement. She saw every surface of her grandmother's face. Though she had deep creases in her cheeks, her skin was smooth, dark brown, glowing. Ruth-Ann's eyes brushed, touched, kissed her grandmother's calm visage, moved to the familiar matting of thick, twisty hair on her head.

Mr. Turner finished introducing Ruth-Ann.

He shook her hand before he took his seat in the front row.

Everybody was clapping.

Ruth-Ann swallowed.

26

She was a little nervous.

She had always earned top marks in elocution and she had memorized her whole speech. She had practiced it many times and Mr. Turner had gone over it carefully with her the two extra days she had spent in school.

Still, she was nervous.

Though she had done many recitations during the church services held in this very building, she had never given a speech that she had written herself to so many grown-ups. She knew, though, that she had done her best to prepare. And people all of her life had told her that her best was very, very good.

She took a deep breath and exhaled slowly.

She began to talk.

The speech came out exactly as she had practiced it except a little better because she was excited. She knew the speech so well that after awhile she forgot about what she was saying. She thought instead, about her mother's mother. Ruth-Ann remembered the day she had gone to Granny-Mame's cabin holding a precious little bundle wrapped in cloth, to share. She had sat down in the dust in front of Granny Mame's steps, and Granny Mame had sat down on the bottom step talking and measuring Ruth-Ann with her eyes.

Ruth-Ann had placed the tiny packet on the step beside Granny-Mame. Carefully, she had unfolded the edges and spread it open.

Granny-Mame had recoiled. She stood and actually backed up two steps, grabbing the railing and thrusting herself away from the little mound of fresh raisins displayed on the checkered cloth.

Ruth-Ann had been shocked. Ashamed at whatever she had done that was so wrong, and hurt, too. She wanted to get next to Granny-Mame, close the distance between them, rush up and hold her.

Granny-Mame had held Ruth-Ann's sobbing face to her bosom. She had held her granddaughter tight and shushed her, telling her not to worry.

"No, girl, don't you cry," she said. "It's jest somethin' comin' back from olden times, times befo' you was born, times I hopes nevuh comes agin. You so sweet to brang yo granny a present."

She patted Ruth-Ann's back and held her, rocking her.

"I'm sorry. I'm so sorry," Ruth-Ann had sobbed. "I didn't mean to do anything wrong."

It all seemed so long ago, Granny-Mame comforting her, and telling her not to worry, that Ruth-Ann had no need to trouble herself over feelings about raisins that came from slavery-times. That mess was all over with.

Granny-Mame had been a young child during slavery times, but her memories of them were vivid. She said colored were not treated like people, "like folk," she said. It was as if they were some kind of animal, like the mules they worked beside in the fields. The overseer did not even talk to them as if they were human. Maybe he spoke, but she did not remember his saying a word. All she remembered was a field horn that was used to communicate with them. She remembered the wailing of that horn like some kind of infernal voice rising up from hell and ruling over her life. They blew it in the morning for wake up. They blew it to signal the time to go to the fields. They called break time with it, and return - feeding and curfew. Always and everywhere the horn was a command, a blaring moan of authority dominating their lives.

"Dey used dat ol' horn t' call usn's ta da feedin's. Jest lak animules."

When she was a slave child she had not known what a plate or a fork were. She and her parents, brothers and sisters, all had worked in the fields. When the horn called them to eat, it called them to a feeding trough, it was exactly the same as the ones which fed the pigs. It was long. They lined either side of it, tightly packed. Then the slave food was poured into it. It went running down from one end to the other until it almost reached the top.

While it was still running down the trough, they used to fight each other for space, and grab, and push and stick their faces in it, trying to get as much as they could, as fast as they could. She remembered the terrible frenzy of those feeding moments.

She never got over the smell of that mess. It stank so bad that if you had not been almost mad with hunger, you could not have forced yourself to gobble it down. They had cows on that plantation, and all the excess milk, all the spoiled milk, was poured into that slave food, along with whatever leavings and garbage were available. But the food got its color from the milk - and a lot of its rancid smell from the bad milk. White, slave food, running as a fetid stream into the trough.

"But, Ruth-Ann," she said, "da flies. Da flies useter come an` set on dat white slave food. Come an` buzz, an` set, an` crawl on dat slave food. Usn's be'd hongry. Flies went down wit all dat mess. Usn's was too busy gittin` ouhas t` push no flies out `n da way. No, ma'am. Ebyday. Ebyday dey come. Look jes lak raisins settin` on dat milk. Jes like raisins.

"Soon as de jubilee done come an` slav'ry times done finished - we done stopped eatin` out'n dat trough - little somethin` what Ah was, Ah swoe - swoe befo` God - Ah never would put no raisins ta mah lips. Never no milk. Ah cain't stand neithuh one ta dis day. Ah's sorry. So sorry, chile. Ah spiled yo` sweet present.

29

Was slav'ry times what done dat ta yo` Granny Mame. Ah kin still smell dat white stink, still heah dem flies buzzin` - still see `em crawlin` on dat milk."

For awhile Ruth-Ann did not understand why all the people were standing and clapping, the older ones shouting, "A-Men!", and some, "Praise Jesus!" Then she realized she had finished speaking. She could not understand how that could account for the tears in so many eyes, the smiles of joy, the faces swollen and beaming with pride.

Afterwards, after all the ceremonies and everybody praising Ruth-Ann and hugging her and kissing her and telling her Mama and Papa over and over what a special child they had, after the social, the cool, sweet tea, and baked treats, the Weatherings did not talk much on the long walk home. Just every now and then Mama or Papa touched a child. The road stretched through the darkness tinted by moonlight. The scent of the great river on its way to the sea filled the evening.

# 6

"Y'all go play outside," said Ruth-Ann's mother. "Go play in that sand outback."

Ruth-Ann laughed.

That is where she had played yesterday, before dark, when they were called in.

She ran out the back door.

The day was so bright and shiny. She didn't remember ever having seen it so bright before.

She laughed.

Across the yard, she could see the sandy area she'd played in yesterday. The sun shone on it, making it look like gold.

Where were her stupid little brothers and sisters?

Mama had not said, "Ruth-Ann." She'd said, "Y'all." "Y'all go play outside."

Where were they?

They weren't with her.

She couldn't even hear them.

Stupid little dumbies.

I don't care.

Let them get in trouble.

I know what Mama told us to do.

She jumped off the porch and ran across the yard. When she reached the sand it felt warm on the bottoms of her feet. She laughed.

She looked for the hole she had dug the night before. She wanted to keep working on it, making it deeper. Maybe she'd dig all the way to China.

Those bad kids were going to get in trouble. They still hadn't come outside.

Ruth-Ann saw the stick she'd been digging with yesterday.

"Ha," she said.

She ran over to it. It was right beside the hole.

Good.

She knelt down. She picked up the stick.

She looked down in the hole. It was deep. She didn't know how she had dug so far. She smiled. Maybe she *could* dig all the way to China.

She saw that some loose sand had fallen into the hole during the night. She decided to scoop it out with her hand before she started digging again. She eased herself over the edge and slid down into the bowl she'd created. She didn't remember it's being so wide and deep.

I forgot my digging stick.

That's alright. I'll climb back up and get it when I've scooped out these few handsfull of loose sand. She bent down and cupped each hand full of sand and hurled it up over the edge of the pit. On the next grab her left hand came up full of dry, loose sand, but that must have been the end of it, because as her right hand sank out of sight, the granules it dug into were tightly packed and moist. There was so little light way down there in the bottom of the chasm she couldn't see her hand. She just felt it sinking into the dense, damp particles.

The tips of her fingers touched something clammy. It squirmed.

Ruth-Ann stood up and screamed but she could not stop herself from grasping the cold, writhing thing.

Hysterical, still screaming, she brought her hand almost to her face so she could see the gelatinous monstrosity convulsed in her involuntary grasp.

Her breath stopped.

It wriggled. Its hind legs kicked, and kicked. Its great mouth opened and closed. Its front legs waved in the air. Her hand, her disobedient hand, would not stop squeezing, squeezing, the mottled, bumpy skin of the hoppy-toad.

Somehow it slipped out of her grip. She saw it falling from her hand into the depths below. It swelled. It metamorphosed before her as it descended. When it stopped falling, it was entirely black. It stood with her alone in the pit, towering above her. It shook its gorgeous black neck, sending its mane flying. It raised up on its hindquarters and raked its forehooves in the air, whinnying madly.

Ruth-Ann woke up screaming.

She screamed and screamed.

She could not stop.

*Spring 1913*

# 7

Calter Harris did not like traveling on the swamp road by himself. He and his brother, Bodell, traveled together wherever they went. Calter was not used to being alone, and the swamp road was not a good place even for one used to solitude. He tried to keep his mind at ease. It was neither the prospect of animals from the swamp nor the specter of hants which bothered him. It was men.

He wished for the easy movement of Bodell beside him. Together they were a formidable pair. Both stood over six feet, four inches tall. Each of them weighed over two-hundred forty pounds, solid as stone. Together they had walked all the roads in the county from sunrise to moonrise, at high noon and deepest dark of night. Together, they feared no man, no hooded fanatic, no band of night riders. Alone, Calter felt the dreadful menace of night.

Bodell had gone to court Maebelle Fletcher after they left work at the mill. That meant Calter had to walk home alone. The loud swamp noises - sometimes piercing cries, sometimes deep grunts - overriding continual small animal sounds of tweets, croaks, and chirps, did not ease Calter's nerves. Still, they were not the sounds he feared. Human voices, the clank of a human implement, the scrape of metal, or the thudding of horses' hooves were what spooked him . He could feel his every sense tuned to the night. He could almost feel each hair on his head, his body, reaching out to monitor the surrounding blackness. He moved, but his whole being was extended, sensitized to detect whatever presence the deep gloom held. Thus, his awareness gave him certain knowledge, before he heard any human sound, that other men had joined him in the darkness.

He knew they were not Black men. No Black men would be out on the road this late, not even the conjur man people said lived in the swamp. The people whose presence he felt were white men.

He stopped. He listened. He could not hear them. He knew any white men had to be behind him, coming the way he had come. This far out, no whites lived up the main road. They would be coming from behind.

The distant clank of metal on metal, alien to the sounds of the living night, was the first sign from the interlopers he heard. It startled him. It confirmed what he already knew, but it was jarring. He moved, settling into a fluid, relaxed run. Scarcely able to see, he glided over the uneven surface in flowing, rhythmic motion. Muscles, speed, and power, he made barely a sound as he sped through the dark.

He coasted to a walk as the swamp road finally penetrated the swamp itself. There blackness was complete. He could see nothing. He walked to the edge of the road where he could feel his way using his feet, and feeling with his hands for large trees along the edge of the road. When he reached a big tree, he would test for low-lying branches. At last he reached a very broad tree with low limbs. He stopped there and began to climb. Thirty feet above the ground, he stretched out flat, on a giant branch, pointed his face in the direction from which the riders had to enter the swamp, and waited.

They came fifteen minutes later. Ten mounted white men carried torches. For being so many, mounted, and carrying a lot of paraphernalia, they made remarkably little noise. Their voices were low, but clear and distinct.

"Jess, you b'lieve what they says 'bout nigga spooks in these hyar swamps?"

"You mean the spooks o' niggas what been lynched out heah?"

"Yeah."

"Hell, Jess don't know nothin' 'bout that. He ain't nevuh killed no nigga."

There was nervous laughter.

"Gon' ter kill one tonight."

More laughter.

"Yeah, but what y'all think 'bout what they says?"

"All I got ter say, some nigga spook come jumpin' out'n these trees, he gon' ter git hisself lynched again!"

They were soon past Calter's place, carrying their own space of fiery light with them.

Calter waited until darkness and silence had settled completely on the swamp, then he swung easily down the tree. He set off after them, keeping the darkness and the silence between them and himself.

They stopped at the fork. When Calter came to the place where the road came out of the swamp, leading to the fork, he could see them seated on their horses in a tight group. He could not hear them. He realized with a sense of misgiving that he would have to get closer to hear. He went to his hands and knees and began crawling rapidly down the road. The darkness and the high grass made it impossible for the men to see him.

When he could hear them, he stopped, flat against the road.

"Wheelock, you sure it's the fust house?"

"Yessuh, fust house off the main road."

"Well Foster, how come you don't agree with him?"

"Now, Ah ain't said Ah disagreed. Ah jest said Ah weren't so sure. Could be further on up the road."

*First house,* thought Calter. *That's our house. They couldn't be talking about the first house.*

"Ain't no futhuh up the road. Ah'll tell you why Ah knows that's the house. Ain't no othuh house 'tween theah and Nightmare's field."

"You right, Wheelock. That's got ter be the one."

"Tha's what Ah tol' you fellers. Don't doubt ol' Wheelock."

"Damn hoss should 'a kilt that nigga bitch."

"Don't worry 'bout that. We gon' ter take care o' the killin'."

"What ef them two, big, buck boys tries to cause some trouble?"

"Well, Ah reckon it'll jest be two, big, buck boys who git theirs a little quicker. But tha's why we got ter git 'em by surprise."

Calter listened in disbelief.

"Gotdamn niggas ought 'ter know better'n treat a white man thataway."

"Gon'ter know better now, by golly . Ev'ry gotdamn nigga in the loop o' the St. Johns - clear up to Mandarin - gonter know bettuh aftuh ternight!"

*There could be no mistake. They meant to attack his house.*

He pushed himself off the ground and stood to his full height. It seemed to take him an hour to stand. Down the road his mother and father slept. He felt his two-hundred and forty pounds shivering in the hot, Florida night.

"White folks!"

"What the hell?"

37

Panic struck the band of killers. The talk of men hanging in the swamp, their bodies intent on revenge, had already unnerved several of them. The voice struck them with pure, agonizing fear. There was no mistaking. It was a nigger voice. Horses and men turned to face up the road. They could not see anything in the darkness. Two shotguns raised and pointed in the direction the voice came from.

One man got enough control over his trembling voice to yell out, "What fool nigger trick is this!"

Calter let them hang in silence.

He was furious and terrified, but he savored their confusion. He watched them.

Then he shouted, "Y'all white folks lookin` fo` two, big nigga bucks name Bodell and Calter Harris?"

"Who is *you*, nigga, and what does you care?"

Calter quietly shifted his position. From his new place, still invisible to the mounted men, he called out, "Well, white folks. *We* is Bodell and Calter Harris. Heah we is. Right heah. An` we been lookin` fo` you!"

"Them niggas is crazy!"

The riders, still unable to see anyone, milled about in confusion.

Calter, having hurled his challenge, turned and sprang toward the swamp, running quietly across the meadow.

One rider, a particularly cruel expression stamped on his face, spun his horse round and round, staring into the faces of his companions, and shouting.

"Is we gon'ter stan` fo` this? Is ten white men gon` ter be faced down by two no-good nigga-bucks? Act like white men, you bastids!"

His anger fused the ragged cabal into action. The horses fanned out into a wide line and charged in the direction the voice had come from. The riders yelled and shouted, several firing blindly ahead of themselves.

To the left of the shouting and discharging flank of riders, Calter gained the refuge of the swamp. He lay still, watching. He could see only the men carrying torches. What he saw was enough to let him understand they didn't know what they were doing.

One group wheeled around and galloped up the road, returning to where they had started their charge. Another bunch followed the road into the swamp. All of them were yelling. Those with guns were shooting them off into the empty dark. None of them were anywhere near Calter.

The riders who had charged off on the swamp road came racing back, still cussing and shooting.

"Shit!"

"Goddamn you assholes!"

"You damn-near kilt me!"

The horsemen came reigning to a halt, disjointedly bumping into each other.

Calter saw one torch-bearer fly off his horse and disappear in the darkness. Calter heard him hit the ground and bounce.

"Help! Help," the man yelled. "My damn brand's got me afire! Oh, help! Oh, help me!"

The man rose to his feet and rushed around, whirling and turning, flames like a brilliant mane running up and down his back. Shadows converged on him and the shadows disappeared in the night's blackness.

"I'm burning! I'm burning!"

"Shet-up, Bedley. We's puttin` it out! We's puttin` it out!"

39

A horseman road up, his torch illuminating him and the riders he joined.

"You bastards damn near shot me."

"Hey, Tom. Didn't nobody mean it. We didn't know nobody stayed in the meadow."

"What the hell do you mean? I'm carryin' a damn torch - got me lit up like the Fourth of July! I bet them niggas ain't got no trouble seein' me."

"We didn't mean nothin'. We was jest tryin' t' shoot the niggas."

"In pitch night. Hell - I was the *only thing* lit up."

"Hey, Tom, we didn't -"

"And what's all that wrestlin' over there? Did somebody catch one o' the niggas?"

"Naw, that's Hankins and Billy. They's puttin' out Bedley's fire."

"Bedley's -"

"Yeah, his horse run inta mine and his own torch caught hisself afire."

"Damn. You is some sorry bastards. How you 'spect t' catch two, big, buck niggers? Burnin' your own damn fool selves up?"

Suddenly, the little knot of men tensed. They could tell that those who had ridden in the other direction had turned around and were returning. They were riding hard, whooping, and still shooting.

"Shit! Let's git off this damn road before they kills us!"

Calter saw the horses lurching into the meadow, the frantic men mounted on them. The three men on the ground ran and stumbled, trying desperately to stay in the light cast by the torches. Spooked and defensive, the horses reared at the staggering shadows. The men, terrified, cried out and hurled themselves back into the oblivion of darkness.

Calter held his sides to keep from bursting out laughing.

The returning group thundered into the crossroad. They pulled their horses to a halt, colliding with each other. One man tumbled out of the saddle, one foot still in the stirrup. A torch fell out of his hand and extinguished itself harmlessly in the damp grass. The other batch of riders, all mounted now, rode out of the meadow and joined those on the road. They argued heatedly about whether they should continue chasing around blindly in the dark, more in danger of killing each other than catching vaporous niggers, or whether they should go on with their objective of attacking the niggers in the cabin down the road.

Calter listened. He knew he had to keep the initiative. He could not let the decisions that were to be made that night fall to them. He stood ten yards from the protective wall of the swamp.

"White folks!"

Again, he sowed anarchy and dissension in their ranks. The men and horses bumbled into each other. There was no immediate prospect of their uniting into a single purpose.

A shot-gun blast ripped off in the direction of Calter's voice. Two riders dashed forward, following the path taken by the shot. One waved an axe, the other brandished a pistol. Another rider geared his mount forward, waving a torch to give them some light. Despite the attempts of some men to stem it, the chase was on. Riders spurred their mounts into the hole of night, lashing out at the empty dark.

One rider sat alone, contemptuously watching the gyrations of his obsessed comrades. It was he who had first shamed them, reminding them they were white men. They had taken all the torches with them. They seemed like clownish dolts to him, careening

41

wildly through flickering splotches of light. He sat engulfed in blackness.

Calter knew the senseless pursuit would soon come to an end. They would gather again, perhaps not to be deterred this time from their assault on his home. He could not let that happen. He moved for the lone rider.

Out of the darkness Calter's strong hands clamped onto the man's ankle and yanked. A high screech rang out of the man's mouth, alerting the wild-eyed vigilantes, scattered in their confused charges.

Calter used all his strength and the weight and momentum of his moving body to jerk the rider out of his stirrups and off the saddle. As the rider came screaming, falling off the horse, Calter kept his grip on his booted leg and they hit the ground together. By then the man was hysterical. In one quick shift of position, Calder had his hands around the man's throat and began pounding his head into the ground. He heard the others coming, and using all his energy drove his giant fist into the shrieking white face, quickly rotating his wrist at the initial impact. Then he scrambled away into the high grass.

The men assembled around their fallen companion. They found him unconscious, his face a bloody pulp. Now driven by a verifiable terror, a mutual desperation directed their actions. They left their friend on the ground and rode swiftly into a wide circle. They turned their horses to trot inward, closing the ring.

Calter, moving cat-like through the grasses, raised his head. He saw he was surrounded. He realized he would have to slip between two of the riders and their little cones of torch-light. As he watched them, he realized the more quickly he acted, the better, because as they moved in, the shrinking circle diminished the spaces between the horses.  Running low he took off for a mid-point between two closing riders.

As he gained speed, Calter wished he could stand up.  He could run much faster that way.  He was by now quite tired so that his breathing was heavy and his movements somewhat labored.  Still, he ran swiftly, quietly, making just a deep panting sound.  As the distance between the two horses narrowed, Calter slightly adjusted his path.

"Frank!  Wheelock!  Ain't that somethin' comin' toward y'all - fast?"

Calter felt heat explode all over him, he swerved in another direction.

"Theah he goes!  Ovuh ter you, Tommy-Lee!"

They were converging on him.  More than one could see him.  He picked out one man, straightened up, and accelerated.

The man tried to turn his horse around, but he did not have the quickness.  Calter was on the horse with him and the man yelled.  The horse reared, whinnying with fright.  He came down bucking, and both men fell off.  The white man flailed, berserk with fear, Calter's bear-like embrace crushing his rib-cage.  As they hit the ground, Calter scanned about him for an escape route.  He saw only the bucking horse and surrounding him the torch-lit faces of angry white men.

He could not get away.  If he held the man as a captive, since they had him in a circle, somebody could get him from behind.  Maybe, he thought, I can get them to make it quick.  He began to ring the neck of the man who sprawled trembling and jibbering beside him.

The flat of an axe struck Calter in the back of the head.  Two shotgun butts drove into his ribs, and a looping chain came swinging

43

up, smashing him across the side of his face.

Calter rose to his feet, turning and swinging his arms about him as he did. Coming up, he knocked over two men. The barrel of a shotgun caught him across the bridge of his nose. An axe handle dug into his solar plexus. The white men shouted to each other. Calter could not understand them. He reached for one swinging a chain at him. Just as Calter's hand locked onto the redneck's wrist, an expression of horror flashed into the man's face. Calter felt the rough fibers of a rope grazing his neck. He jammed his free hand up to get it between the rope and his neck. The man who had thrown the rope, yanked back on it, wrapped two turns around his pommel, then wheeled his horse and kicked him into flight.

The horse's powerful surge tore Calter off his feet, but he had managed to get his hand between the rope and his neck. He held tightly to the rope. Nor did his other hand lose its hold on the imprisoned wrist.

The white men rushed to stop the galloping rider. They were unable to communicate to him why he must stop. It took a while for him to realize they were desperate for him to rein in. He turned his horse abruptly. He was shocked to see in the torchlight, not one figure on the ground, but two, and one of them white. Incredibly, the black body began to stand.

My God, thought Harker. Maybe this *is* some kind o` nigga spirit from the swamp. Ain't nothin` human that strong. It should be dead. My God, look at the size o` that buck.

The black figure dragged the white one up with it.

The riders argued with each other. There were supposed to be two niggers. They had only one. Someone had let the other one get away.

44

Calter felt enough pleasure at their bewilderment to smile through his pain. He raised his voice.

"You don't need to keep no lookout fo` my brothuh, cause he keepin` a lookout on you."

His words upset his captors even more. They were torn between shooting Calter down where he stood - which was the end for which he so fervently wished - and rushing out to find the other nigger who lurked in the dark. Meanwhile the man in Calter's grip gained consciousness and pleaded for his companions to release him.

Calter turned to his prisoner and tightened down on his wrist.

"Say please, white man."

"Oh! Nigga! Nigga ... oh - oh, please. Please! PLEASE!"

The man with the rope around Calter could not stand to see the degradation of a member of the white race. He turned his horse and dragged Calter off his feet again. He pulled him ten yards.

Before Calter could get to his feet, one rider had dismounted, driving a gun butt into Calter's hand, freeing his captive.

Calter felt rope going around his feet. He tried to kick free, but it was taught, the pull of a horse at the other end. He had now just the one free hand, numb from the blow of the rifle butt. They had him turned on his back.

The men were all down from their horses. They surrounded Calter. They cursed him and reviled him. They spelled out in cruel detail what they were going to do to him. They raged at him for messing up their night. It was too late, now, to ride on to his parents' house. His brother, they feared, would alert them. They would have to vent all their rage on him. He would pay.

"Y'all actually had the nerve to go to the front do` of a white man's house!"

"An` ask fo` that whiteman t` come to the do` t' see you!"

45

"Shut up, Slim! Ah'm tellin` this.

"Nervy niggas. Walk right up to the do` of a white man, and say you ain't goin` ter no back do`, and he got ter answer you at the front do` like you was white folks. Goddman! Ah gits mad jest thinkin` about it. You bastids!"

"Ah don't care how many little nigga bitches got killed or almost killed by a white man's hosses or dogs or any othuh goddamn thing. You understand me! The little bitch wasn't even killed. Should'a been. You gon'ter wish she was, gon'ter wish you nevuh heard o` her when we gits through with you."

"Say yo` Daddy even had the nerve to threaten - threaten! A nigga threaten! Threaten that if Cooper didn't catch that hoss, he was gon'ter kill it.

"Y`all lost all yo` sense that day. And now you gon` ter pay fo` it. You gon ter teach a lesson t` all the niggas from heah to Fort George!"

They were not swift with their vengeance. They were not kind. Each man had a special madness to contribute to the ghastly work.

Calter remembered the sparkle of stars in the black sky.

*Summertime* 1913

# 8

There was no way to hide what had happened to Calter, not even from the children. Not the way they left his body.

By the talk that circulated through the little settlements and scattered houses, there could be no doubt about why white folks had done it. As colored talked among themselves many came to question the Harrises' behavior. It would have been just as easy to go to the back door. The results for capturing Nightmare would have been the same. Hadn't Mr. Cooper gathered up all the men and boys he could to corral him? Didn't he do it right away? He would have done the same thing if they'd gone to the back door. Charlie had tried to warn them. But, no, they let their anger make them big-headed, specially Mr. Harris. The boys were just following their father. Look at what it got them. Look at the danger it brought to every Negro in the county. Folks had to learn how to act. A lot of people felt that way, but not everybody. Some were proud of the Harrises and said, "It's about time." But everybody was terrified.

The Weatherings felt worst of all, especially Ruth-Ann. But Mr. Harris walked all the way to her house to tell her not to feel bad.

"It weren't yo' fault, Ruth-Ann. "I. That's the way I raised my boys up. To be men." He walked her out in the yard. "I would o` made a bad slave. If these was slavery times, they would o` kilt me a long time ago. I don't believe a human bein` was made t'be a slave. That's how I taught my boys. That's the way I prayed they'd live. Like men. That's the onliest way I knows how t`live - like a

47

man.

"In this heah country that mean - sometimes - you got t`die like one. Befo` yo` time. Befo` yo` time. Like my boy Calter."

He touched her shoulder. "But what I wants you t'understan`, Ruth-Ann, is it weren't `cause o` you. It were `cause o` him. Calter. Who he were. He were a man. A Black man. That's why he had to die like he done. Cause he couldn't live with hissef as no less than a man.

"Do you understan` me, girl?"

She was crying.

He put his arm around her shoulders.

"If it wasn't you with that hoss, it would o` been somebody else. We would o` ended up doin` the same thing. He's a killer. A killer hoss. He have killed befo`. Where you think he got his name? We said it's time to end this thing.

"Calter didn't die `cause o` you, Ruth-Ann. He died `cause the only way he could live was like a man.

"You wasn't out on that road with no shotguns and knives and chains. You wasn't no night-rider out makin` death while decent folk was asleep. You wasn't nothin` but a girl tryin` t` walk t` school."

His eyes were watering, too, but she didn't see them. Her eyes were closed and she was alone in the dark with her pain. She could feel the salt water on her face. That's all she felt except the pain inside.

She leaned into Mr. Harris and wept.

\*

Mr. Harris sounded convincing and Ruth-Ann wanted to

48

believe him. Her parents were solicitous, too, and they said much the same thing. But when she had time alone and could think about it - truth is, she thought of little else - she could not help believing that had she not been on the road that morning, Calter would still be alive and he and Bodell the handsomest brothers in the county.

When people looked at her they knew she was responsible for Calter's death. She could not stand the pain of every day. She could not bear her guilt steeped so deep in every person she saw. She was shattered by the way her presence attached to her family. Shunned. They were shunned. There were people who would not speak to them, not exchange a simple greeting. *For what I did, for my actions. I brought this on myself.* They had nothing to do with it. I'm the one who did it. Only I can set it right.

It took Ruth-Ann several months, much wrestling with herself, changing her mind, staying out of sight. She had graduated from the eight grade, and it was time for her to take responsibility for herself. She had to think about how she was going to live her life - not only what was right - but also how to *do* what was right. As summer came to an end, she knew what she had to do. It was the hardest thing she had ever faced. Nobody wanted her to go. Her brothers and sisters cried and pleaded with her not to go. Her parents told her there was no need to leave. But none of them had to live her life, and none of them could live it for her. Even so, she could not do what she must do without help. She reached out to family ties. She went East to the big city, to Jacksonville, to hide, and to make her own way.

She got work as a nurse-maid to two children at the home where her great aunt, Nidi, worked as a cook to the Fleetwrights, and where Nidi's husband, Ross, was the chauffeur. They became her anchors in a time of troubles.

# 9

Her early months in Jacksonville, Ruth-Ann had to adjust not only to being away from her family, her home, the only place she had ever lived, and to a new household, her place in it, and to the whole re-orientation of becoming a nurse-maid and paid employee. She had to do it in an alien world. Jacksonville was a city. It was nothing like Mandarin. It was a world she wouldn't have believed existed, even if someone had told her about it.

Learning to live in Jacksonville also meant learning to meet new people, to make new friends. She'd never had to make friends. Her friends were the children she grew up with. They'd always been in her life. Meeting people she didn't know - letting them into her life, and going into theirs - was something entirely different. She was, at first, reluctant, timid. But Ruth-Ann liked people and got along with them easily. Nevertheless, she'd been living in Jacksonville and working at the Fleetwrights' for a year before she felt confident that the next day would not be an insurmountable challenge. As she became more comfortable with the routine of daily life, she realized she knew very little about the teeming population of Jacksonville. She had fled Mandarin, not to get away from it, but to distance herself from the dreadful horror she'd brought to it. Somehow, she believed, she had caused Calter's death and the mutilation of his body which had accompanied it. She sobbed herself to sleep many nights, only to enter a land of nightmares.

50

Her flight had deprived her of a future. It was a long time before she recalled Mr. Turner's words, that she was ... *an unusual girl with unusual gifts*. Hearing that had terrified her, yet stirred her heart. Not long afterwards, he had said, *I would recommend that you get her to the Colored high school in Jacksonville.* She was now in Jacksonville - the location of that colored high school. Somewhere in this city - colored students were going to high school. *I could have been one of them. Once upon a time.*

# 10

After the long time it took for Ruth-Ann to get settled at the Fleetwrights, some Saturdays when Mrs. Fleetwright wanted to keep the children herself, Nidi took Ruth-Ann to the market. All the farmers brought their goods to market on Saturday. Nidi and Ross took the wagon every Saturday and filled it up with food for the Fleetwrights. They spent all day at the market, though the shopping only took them two hours. They spent the rest of the time socializing with other Colored people, especially from their home plantations.

Even when it rained, Saturday market was brilliant and sparkling. Laughter, greetings, and vending calls rang from one row of stalls to the next. People haggled over prices skillfully and joyfully. Part of the wonder of the market was coming together. For many it was also anticipating the coming evening - Saturday night.

Often as not, on Monday mornings Nidi had to return for items she'd forgotten. During the summer of Ruth-Ann's second year in Jacksonville, Nidi and she often walked to Monday market. Mondays, Ross was off with Mr. Fleetwright and couldn't bring the wagon. The settled woman and her great niece carried back the necessary odds and ends they'd purchased in their market baskets, balancing them on their heads.

Though the Monday markets were not the holiday of Saturday, they were lively enough. Folks had a chance to discuss the happenings of the weekend. They recounted escapades and adventures of Saturday night. They retold the hell-fire sermons, the dazzling church songs, and the spirit movings of Sunday morning church services. Monday market was not Saturday market, but it had a life of its own.

The crowds were smaller - both vendors and buyers. And whereas on Saturday everyone who made the last Saturday was likely to be there the next and every other Saturday, on Mondays the faces were prone to change. As a result, the exchanges, though warm, were not as familiar.

After they had picked up all the essentials, Ruth-Ann liked to wander among the stalls and carts, before rejoining Nidi for the walk home. She liked to look at the catches in from the river and ocean, to smell the fresh flowers, to touch the fruit and see the beautiful faces of her people, colors of ebony and copper, gold and deep mahogany, colors of ocean sands and summer dawns, colors of midnight, beautiful beyond believing, laughter and sound, rich and resounding. She loved to stop, talk to someone she knew, or smile at a stranger and receive a smile in return.

One Monday morning she saw a man's profile thirty feet away. He was standing next to a cart piled with fresh melons. His long, graceful fingers were spread lightly on a honeydew.

She stopped. He was tall and slender. Dark. He was dark as soft night against the glow of the moon. His features were all fine, clean lines, sharp and well-defined. As he talked, he smiled, dazzling brilliance in the morning light. He was dressed in a smart dark coat and trousers, high starched collar, dark tie. He wore a top hat and doffed it when he turned to move. His movement was like an eagle wheeling in the sky.

She wanted never to stop seeing him. She ran around the rows, cut down the aisle to where he stood, but he had vanished.

*

Minding the children, suddenly Ruth-Ann would see in her mind's eye the man from the market and it was as if the children spoke a foreign language. She would see the stranger's fingers spread out over the melon and the flash of his smile. Whenever she was out on the street, she looked for him. Walking the children. On an errand. Her eyes found every Black man within their reach, but the man who moved like an eagle was not among them.

She twisted and manipulated and turned and squeezed her time and the children's, too, all to be available for visits to the market with Nidi. Once there, she was useless. She could not help with marketing but went wandering through the stalls in search of her man. She did not know how to pray about such a thing. How do you pray about a man, for a man?

She had never given two-cents worth of thought to boys. Some were cute, alright, and she liked to flirt and laugh with them. But it was nothing she spent any time thinking about. At home some of them had wanted to sport her and she had known it, but she laughed at them because she wasn't studdin` about them. In Jacksonville, some of the boys were very nice and a few so handsome she had to smile when she saw them. But she was much too busy to be more than amused by them. Perhaps the most important thing about the man in the market was that he was not a boy. He was a man for sure and Ruth-Ann saw him as she had never seen any boy. The day she saw him, she'd wanted to run to him and hold him, kiss him, never let him go.

She had never before in her life wanted to kiss anyone - in that way. But she felt if she could just kiss him he would be hers

54

forever and ever. She wanted that now even more than she wanted to breathe, because if she didn't have him, she didn't want to breathe. She knew no way to ask about him, to inquire after him. She didn't know his name. She didn't know where he lived or worked. There had been just that instant when she had seen through the vendors and there he was.

*If I don't see him again I will die.*

She railed against the thought that he was just an illusion, some figment of her imagination. That could not be true. She refused to believe it could be true. Yet every time she reached the place where she believed he had been, he was not there, nor was he anywhere within her vision.

# 11

When Ruth-Ann thought about home, she imagined she saw the main room of their house with Mama and Papa, Naomi, Paul, Wilma, and Jason all gathered around their little table. Their stomachs were full and Papa was telling tales his Mama had told him from slavery times. Granny-Mame was there and she'd correct Papa every now and then.

"For I were there," she reminded him. "I done seed it wid my own eyes. Yessuh."

He went on and after awhile Granny-Mame would say, "Folks come up after it, ain't seen nothin' like it. Y'all don't know."

Mama put her arms around Granny-Mame and the two of them sat in the shadow just out of reach from the flicker of the coal-oil lamp.

The family might even sing a song or two. If it were a work song, Daddy would lead it with everybody filling in on the choruses.

*"Well, I'm gwine t' chop me a line,*
*Huyallup, Huyallup.*
*Yes, I'm gwine t' chop me a line,*
*Huyallup, Huyallup.*
*Gwine t' make my pay from the section boss,*
*Huyallup, Huyallup.*
*An' be the first t' dance t' the banjo-time,*
*Huyallup, Huyallup.*

How they'd laugh. Papa made up his verses as he went along and always found a way to fit them with a rhyme. If it were a spiritual, Mama would lead.

After awhile the little ones would go to bed. Those who stayed up kept talking. Gradually, all the children went to bed. Only the adults remained in the oscillating sphere of light. Their voices droned on - sometimes sprinkled with laughter.

Lying in the dark, Ruth-Ann loved that sound.

Except this year she would not be there, as she had not been the year before.

*Summer of 1915*

# 12

The Fourth of July was a big celebration for everyone, Colored and white. They did not celebrate together, but for both peoples it was a great occasion. For Colored it was great largely because after they had made the preparations for the whites' festivities - except for those who were actually serving- they had the rest of the day off. In Jacksonville, that meant all the help got together for a great picnic.

Ruth-Ann was alive with excitement. Even though, way out in the country, she had heard about Jacksonville's Colored Fourth of July picnic, she had not attended the past year because the holiday was a family occasion that required her presence at the white picnic with the Fleetwrights' children. Now, the children were old enough to accompany their parents without her.

The Colored picnic grounds were on a broad expanse of grass that lay right on the river. Several ancient live oaks spaced about the sunlit field formed pools of shadow. Ruth-Ann was dizzied by the excitement. Nidi chaperoned Ruth-Ann and her friends.

Everyone dressed finely, in their brightest, boldest things. Some young women wore their white, frilly blouses, and trim bodices, with long elegant skirts reaching the ground. They turned, petticoats whirled, buttoned shoes peeped out. Some wore greys, blacks, and browns. Here and there someone sported flashes of red, of yellow, green, orange or blue. Their hats were marvels - decorated with ribbons, flowers, and great, wide, lazy brims.

The laughter ringing from their throats was like the tinkling of high, light bells. Many had spread out gay cloths - checked - reds and whites and blues, intricate prints of myriad colors. Foods were displayed as irresistible offerings - piles of fried chicken, roast pork, bowls of dark beans and white rice, dishes of greens and rhubarb, peach and apple cobblers, fruit platters of grapes, plums, pears, peaches, rasberries, blackberries. There were freshly baked biscuits, corn bread, and hoppin' john. Delicious aromas drifted over the grounds.

Young men strutted about in groups of two and three. They gestured eloquently, struck poses, laughed reservedly, smiled often, and cast the most outrageous glances in the direction of the ladies.

Braced against a massive oak, a tempting potpourri of offerings spread out before them on a wildly exotic cloth, Ruth-Ann and her friends, Essie and Lavinia, giggled uncontrollably. Ruth-Ann drank in Essie's dark beauty, her finely etched features. Lavinia's boisterous presence, her high-yellow loveliness framed in long, auburn ringlets and her broad, prominent features, set up the two as distinct contrasts in types. She loved them.

"Oh, girl," said Ruth-Ann, "I must be dreaming. I've never seen anything like this."

Nidi pontificated about all the Fourth of July celebrations she'd seen, how many grand, how many glorious. She compared them with each other, and with the current one. She explained how this one differed, and how it was similar. How people dressed, how they carried themselves, the food they prepared, all became subjects of her discourse. Her monologue was continually interrupted by clusters of young gallants, stunned by the beauty gathered under the tree - seeking to stun in turn. The dashing gentlemen made polite conversation, tasted delicacies from the courses spread on the cloth, engaged in wild flirtations with their eyes. Group after group found a way to pass by the tree again.

The girls were intoxicated by it all. Between entourages, when Nidi took a breath, they engaged in feverish and slightly lightheaded reflections on the last party to pass by, on some cherished favorite or some unmitigated fool.

By late afternoon Nidi had tired of the endless procession of dandies. Interesting at first, several hours of it had grown wearisome for her. She groaned at the approach of another trio.

"Don't these young'uns ever git tired o` this," she complained.

Lavinia's reaction was opposite. She prepared to smile and lower her eyes coquettishly.

Ruth-Ann cast a glance at the oncoming men.

*The world started spinning crazily.*

The man at the market.

Older than his companions. More defined. It was as if he stood apart from them. She had seen him for only an instant, but she could never, never forget him. She seemed to lose the power of speech. She could feel her heart pounding through all her ruffles and lace. She had known, she had known all along. He had not been imaginary.

The men paid their respects to Nidi.

Ruth-Ann stared at him, close now.

*Who is this that cometh out of the wilderness like pillars of smoke, perfumed with myrrh and frankincense ....*

They doffed their hats. His hair like his skin was black,

except there was a slight aura of copper in its cast. It was curly, wavy hair, brushed back along his head in soft, running waves. His dress was elegant. Every line seemed tailored to his sharp, aristocratic features. He carried himself with great dignity. She could not think. She could hear only the song of songs ringing in her ears.

*Let him kiss me with the kisses of his mouth; for thy love **is** better than wine.*

Ruth-Ann heard not a word exchanged between Nidi and the men. She did see Nidi turn, and heard her say,

"Gentlemens, I'd like t` introduce you to three young ladies who is the flower of Jacksonville. Next t` me this is Miss Essie Grey, and the middle one is Miss Ruth-Ann Weathering, and next to her, Miss Lavinia Watson."

All three girls curtsied.

The men bowed. Then each introduced himself.

Ruth-Ann did not hear what the first one said. The middle one, the stranger, the man she would never forget, said,

"I am most honored and pleased to make your acquaintances, ladies. Of course, I know Lavinia." He smiled at her, Lavinia smiled back, dropping her eyes. A fury of jealously seized Ruth-Ann. "My name is Stephen Wenders." He spoke to Ruth-Ann alone. He did not take his eyes off of her.

The last one said his piece, but Ruth-Ann did not hear him. She looked at the one she loved and heard, *Stay me with flagons, comfort me with apples; for I **am** sick of love.*

When they had moved on, Lavinia thrust her face at her friends and exclaimed, "Did you see Stephen Wenders look at Ruth-Ann?"

Essie laughed. "Did you see Ruth-Ann look at Stephen

61

Wenders?"

"Why," said Ruth-Ann. "What did I do?"

"What did you do," burst in Nidi. "Evuhthing but jump up an' hug him. You didn't take yo' eyes offen dat man."

"Hmm," said Lavinia, "I missed that, but I know those Wenders. They come from out my way."

"What about them? What do you know," demanded Ruth-Ann.

"They're all crazy, that's all," said Lavinia. "There are ten or twelve of them and all just plain crazy. They're all real smart. Too smart. There's such a thing as being too smart. The Wenders - well - I wish there was another word for smart, because that's what they are - too smart. And when you cross that line - get too smart - you're crazy. That's the Wenders. All smart. Past smart. Crazy.

"And beautiful, too. Just like Stephen. All of them so handsome they make you want to cry. But crazy! The women are just like the men - beautiful and crazy. Stephen's just as smart as the rest of them, I hear," said Lavinia. "He must be as crazy, too. Those surely are some beautiful crazy people, though. I could almost put up with some craziness to stay with a man like that."

"I'm going to marry that man," said Ruth-Ann.

The three other women looked at her. They burst into an uncontrollable fit of laughter.

## 13

Though Stephen Wenders' tastes were decidedly urban, his early life at his family's country home had ruined him for life in the city. That ruination had nothing to do with the differences between urban and rural living, where - for Stephen - urbanity won out hands-down. It had everything to do with freedom.

Stephen associated life on his family's place with labor - arduous, physical labor. He seemed to be born with a broom, mop, shovel, trowel, axe, peeling or skinning knife, basket, rope, scrub brush, hammer, saw, hoe, rake, or chisel, in his hands. He could hunt anything, catch every kind of fish, exterminate any varmit, and knew poultices for every kind of insect bite. But all that knowledge and accompanying sets of skills were lost on him.

He loved being freshly bathed. Fastidious, he was a bit of a dandy. He wanted to dress up and strut around like a rooster. That's really the reason he went to church, and to the little country school the few times it was open during his youth - to show off, and more importantly - to be seen.

He was not, however, lazy. The work he loved to do was not with his body, but with his mind. In the country, while the mind was in constant use, it was always closely linked to the labors of the body. The two were intrinsically bound. That was a bondage Stephen wanted to break.

If he remained on the Wenders homestead, he'd never break it. The few weeks - over a period of years - he'd spent in school, opened his mind as if he'd lived in a closet before. It was there, in a terribly brief time, that he'd learned to read and do figures. The experience ripped away veils that had hung over the world, and exposed him to the wonder of existence and the joys of complex thinking.

Once he learned to read, he read the bible so many times he almost memorized it. He read, literally, everything he could get his hands on. He worked figures whenever he could. They fascinated him, like a game. He was happy to do Papa's figuring to relieve him from that part of his labors. He wasn't lazy, but what he wanted to work with lay between his ears.

That's what got him rooting around to find out if there were some place where a Black man could get himself some education - and to the high school for Colored in Jacksonville. It went through the tenth grade. At first, he didn't believe it. He was hoping to find a Colored elementary school that was up and running every year. He'd had no idea there was a high school for Colored people anywhere. To think there was one as close as Jacksonville made him a little drunk. He was eighteen years old when he heard about that high school. Right then, he fixed his mind on how he was going to get into it.

# 14

Stephen always seemed strange to Tims and Solders. But they figured that was his prerogative, as he was the oldest. When he developed his fascination about going to high school, that seemed the strangest of all to them.

"Now, why he want t` do a thing like that," Tims asked Solders one day. "Don't he know that life on Papa's place is as good as it can get?"

"Don't ask me. You the number two brother. I'm only number three. If you really wants to know, why don't you ask Naomi, she ain't but a year younger than him."

"I would. If she ever came back from Jacksonville."

They both laughed.

"You know she ain't comin' back," said Solders. "Papa would tan her hide."

"Sho would," agreed Tims. "His oldest gal gone off to live by herself in the big city."

"That's right," said Solders. "It ain't as if she was white."

They both cracked up.

Whenever they got a chance, they teased their older brother about "puttin` on airs," and wanting to go to Jacksonville like his sister.

That's what gave Stephen the idea to talk with Naomi.

Living right there in Jacksonville, she might be just the right one to find out how he could get into that school.

Though Naomi lived right up in the middle of Jacksonville, she had not the slightest interest in attending the Colored high school. She was much more set on ensconcing herself in the city's Colored social life - or more accurately - not to move an inch from the place where the first sight of her had driven the city's Colored swains so crazy that they were ready to steal, shoot, and kill each other over the chance to be the first each day to say, "Dee Do?" to her - morning, afternoon, or evening.

*

When Stephen visited Naomi in Jacksonville, to learn all he could about that high school, just as she had intended, her friends were properly impressed by her handsome, articulate, and impeccably dressed older brother.

For his part, Stephen was stunned. As he took her by the elbow and guided her outside to the formal garden, he was at first dumbfounded, unable to speak. They walked in silence, she slightly curious about why he wanted to take her away from the gaiety of the party into the stately, but deserted garden. At last, he stopped, and turned to face her.

"Naomi ... all this. Your coiffeur, your couture ...."

"You're quite a hit, big brother," she said.

Stephen shrugged off the comment, "I hardly think so," he said. "But. But. My point is ... *you*. You - are ... so elegant, so cultured, your dress ...."

"Beautiful, isn't it?

"Stephen, what do you think of my hat, my earrings?"

"Naomi ....

"Naomi - how do you afford it? How do you *do* this?

"Where's the money ...."

"Coming from?" She helped him.

"Yes." He dropped his head.

She laughed.

"Now, Stephen Wenders. Stephen. Look at me."

He raised his head and met her eyes.

She took one of his hands, and continued their walk, moving side by side.

"Stephen, you don't believe, do you, I could have lived *and worked*. Yes, *and worked* all that time out in the wilderness with Mama Ona and never learned anything useful?"

"I don't know. I mean, that's the country. This is the city."

"It sho` `nuff is," she said, teasing him. "And you don't yet know, big brother, how much it is."

"But." He stopped. "Look at you. Listen to you. There's nothing out there in the country - like this."

She spun around this time, facing him.

"I'm a seamstress, Stephen. I sew very well. I sew for a first-class establishment. I left for Jacksonville sewing every bit as well as I do right now - from our Mama Ona."

Stephen was shocked.

He saw his sister anew.

He saw his home - way back in the country - anew.

He sighed, relaxed, and smiled.

He squeezed her hands.

"Baby sister." He threw his head back and laughed out loud.

She squeezed his hands and returned his smile. "This frock,

for example,"she said, "which you have so graciously complimented me on - I made myself from remnants - the hat - I made myself. The earrings ... are a gift." She winked at him.

"Which reminds me, that occasionally, Papa sends me an envelope. That helps immeasurably."

Stephen's jaw dropped.

"Papa?"

"I'm sure," she said, "Mama knows about it. What happens out there that she doesn't know?

"Still. He's a shrewd man. Anyway -"

"Papa," he repeated.

"Papa. Yes. You understand, don't you, that as disappointed and as disapproving as he is about my packing up and taking off for Jacksonville, he could not bear the thought of *his daughter*, throwing herself on the mercy of some man - some *common man*?"

"No. No, I didn't. I didn't know ...."

"He loves me, Stephen. He loves all of us. That's the answer."

"Now, Stephen, tell me why you're so set on going to high school."

\*

Naomi played the dutiful sister. She got all the information she could about that high school and how to get into it and forwarded it to her older brother.

Once he knew the course he had to follow, Stephen's first problem was how he was going to make a living in Jacksonville. He'd have to support himself and go to school. How was he going to do that? It was clear to him, that one way or another, he was going to have to find a way to swallow a whole lot of pride - and become a servant. Life on the Wenders homestead had ruined him for any such eventuality.

The Wenders were lords and masters of their hundreds of acres and the stretches of the Saint Johns that flowed past them. Most white people stayed clear of their lands and river banks because they didn't know who they were - or - what they were. There were the white Wenders and the Black Wenders. The white Wenders were powerful people in Duval County, so powerful that most whites did not know there were Black Wenders - the white Wenders didn't want them to. The Black Wenders were products of the male white Wenders' fornications. That was nothing to put on a billboard and parade around the county.

Another reason whites stayed away from the Black Wenders' territory was that some of it had been Indian land, Seminole. The Seminoles were fierce. They had never been defeated. Nobody wanted to mess with them, and if that land was still theirs, the best thing was just to keep clear of it. In a sense, it *was* still Seminole land. The Seminoles were a strange mix of people. At first, there were the Creek Indians. Some of them got mixed up with Africans who had escaped slavery. The Creeks, Africans, and their mixed progeny lived together. People called them after the Cimmarons, Spanish for, "the wild ones," the escapees, the same word which gave the name "Maroons" to settlements of self-freed Africans. Seminole was a bastardization of Cimmaron, a homonym, which attached itself to these Indians, Africans, and mixed people in the wilds of Northern Florida. The Black Wenders' heritage consisted not only of whites and Africans, but Indians, too - Seminoles. So those who feared the territory was Indian land were not entirely

69

wrong. The up shoot of all of that was that the Black Wenders saw few white people. Those they did see were mostly family, someone who came by to see a half-brother, a cousin, a son, a granddaughter or grandson. Once they were on Black Wenders' lands, they stopped acting like members of a master race and started acting like kin-folk. But even they were rare visitors, as the white Wenders had no interest in celebrating the fringe elements of their large family. Among other things, this meant that the sons and daughters of Mama and Papa Wenders acted like princes and princesses as a matter of course. They acted that way because that is how they thought about themselves. Jacksonville was a harder reality.

*

The white man looked at the nigger standing in front of him with his hat in his hands. He didn't like the way the nigger was dressed. Not niggerish enough. He didn't like the way he stood, not enough slump to him.

*He looks too clean to me, and his hair's not knotted up enough for a proper nigger appearance. He gets on my nerves,* thought the man.

"What you say yo` name was, boy?"

"Stephen, sir. Stephen Wenders."

*Got-damn, the nigger pronounce his words too clear.*

"Where you from, boy?"

"Out in the country, sir. Way up on the St. Johns."

"My God, boy, where you learn t'talk like that?"

"Sir?"

"Who taught you to say your words that way?"

70

"Well, sir, I guess my Mama and Papa did."

"You guess?"

"Well, sir, I can't rightly think who else it could o` been."

"Well, yo` mama and papa must be some o` them fancy niggers - not too bright, though. You `bout as dark as they come."

That was the only thing right about the nigger. He was dark as sin.

"Ah tell you what, nigger. You come back here in a year or two when you's learned how t` be a proper nigger, and I might think about takin` you on. But for now - git on outa here and don't let the door hit yo` back."

As Stephen walked away, he thought that if the man had talked to his father that way, his father would have killed him. That's why he lived so far out in the country. So white people wouldn't tempt him to murder them everyday.

But Stephen was not his father. He wanted to go to the Colored high school. But before he did that, he'd have to find a way to live and work in the city. He didn't know how he was going to do that. He was used to being a free man, and white people didn't seem to have freedom in mind for him.

\*

Stephen got thrown out of a lot of places before anyone would take him on. Perhaps the continual and mean-spirited rejections put a little more slump in his shoulders, bowed his head some. Perhaps he got so tired his feet dragged a bit. Perhaps it was all that and just running into a white man here and there who wasn't as mean as the others. Whatever the reasons, after a long time of

71

looking, he finally found some work. His first jobs in Jacksonville were as a porter for small businesses. He cleaned up, scrubbed floors, washed windows, kept the walkways clear, held doors, carried packages, made deliveries. People could see he was a quick study and soon increased his responsibilities. He was happy to have the work, but it was hard to come by.

Unlike looking for a job and holding onto it, finding lodgings was easy. There were many places where Colored lived, and always a Colored person eager to rent-out some shed, closet, or corner of a room. Beyond that, many of the business owners consented to let a porter sleep in the back room, storeroom, sometimes in a shack out behind the business. They felt good about having somebody on the premises when the building was closed. Since the porter stayed at no cost, it was cheaper than hiring a night watchman. It was like having a watch dog. When Stephen made that recognition, he realized his status. He was a dog. He certainly was not a human being. At night, he was a watch dog. During the day, he was a working dog.

# 15

When the Fourth of July was over, Ruth-Ann tried to learn everything she could about Stephen Wenders. Essie and Lavinia sent out runners to all their friends around Jacksonville.

He had come from the country, but he no longer lived in the country. He had come to Jacksonville to seek his fortune. He had not found fortune, but he became skilled as a cook, a butler, and a chauffeur. Because of his grace, his manners, his elegance, his impeccable diction, he was in great demand as a servant, and had served some of Jacksonville's finest families.

Because he had the option, he had lately been working only for families who spent summers in the North and wintered in Florida. Among other things, he was interested in living in various parts of the country and he believed choosing his employers carefully was a grand way to do it. He had shown up at the Fourth of July picnic only because he was between jobs and going through Jacksonville on the way to spend time with his family. Friends had convinced him to stay in Jacksonville for the picnic.

The Colored women in Jacksonville had been crazy over him since he'd first appeared, but he had never married. He had kept company with several stunning women. A few had asked him to marry them, but he had politely declined and had never himself proposed to anyone. He was, the reports went, a confirmed bachelor.

We'll see about that, thought Ruth-Ann. She began writing

out her name so she would get used to seeing it. *Ruth-Ann Wenders.*

She loved the sight of it.

She loved the sound of it.

She said it over and over again.

The problem, she was quite aware, was how to see him again. She was afraid he would evaporate out of her life as he had before.

*No. Not a second time.*

But what was she to do?

\*

Stephen Wenders had wanted to know right away who Ruth-Ann Weathering was, and where she lived. All anyone could tell him was that Nidi knew her, that Essie Grey had given a wonderful birthday party for her, and that Lavinia Watson was a good friend of hers. Those tidbits laid out Stephen's tasks. When he got home, he made a side-trip to call on Lavinia Watson. He had the good luck to find her at home with her family. Stephen and Lavinia sat on the front porch, Stephen on the railing and Lavinia on the swing.

"What can you tell me about Miss Weathering?"

"Oh, Stephen, you're so earnest. Has cupid put an arrow through your heart?"

"Where's she from?"

"She's a country girl - like me. Country. Like you, Stephen."

"Where?"

"Her people are from over around Mandarin. In that backwoods swamp country over theah."

"Mmmm. What's she like?"

"I can tell you one thing. She's too young for you."

74

"What's that? How old is she?"

"Fifteen."

Stephen dropped his eyes.

He looked back at Lavinia.

"Fifteen, you say?"

She laughed.

"Fifteen. Two years younger than I am. But I must admit, Stephen, she's a mature fifteen - and smart as a whip."

He twirled his hat in his hands, watching it spinning.

"Reads everything," said Lavinia.

"How do you think she'd take to my calling on her?"

"She's fifteen, Stephen - fifteen!"

He laughed. "She won't be fifteen forever. I'll be able to look her up every six months and see if she's aged sufficiently."

"For what?"

"That's for me to know and you to find out. You haven't answered my question."

"It would depend," pronounced Lavinia, "on what your intentions were." She smiled, teasing, "whether they were honorable."

Stephen showed his teeth. "But they were all, all honorable men."

"Then you, too, are an honorable man, Stephen?"

"I am."

"As were 'yon Cassius' and Brutus?"

"Lavinia -"

"I ask only because the country may soon go to war, and all able bodied young men - especially Negro men here in the South - may be drafted into the army. Men. Men going off to war have been known to do desperate things to take advantage of innocent young

75

women."

"Not honorable men."

This time Lavinia smiled.

"That, Stephen, is why I asked the question."

Stephen took her hands. He was serious.

"This war - if it comes - will not be my war. The key thing you said, Miss Watson, is *young* men. I am too old for this war. It will not be my war."

"Too old for war, but not too old for a fifteen year old girl?"

"As I said. She will not be fifteen forever. I ... one of the virtues of increased age is patience. I can wait. My intentions are honorable."

He released her hands, patted them, and smiled again.

"Smile for me again, Stephen. Smile for me again and I'll tell you anything."

He laughed.

"Girl, you haven't changed."

"Should I? I can't imagine why I should ever change."

"Nor can I."

"Well," she said, "since you smiled for me, not really, though. Actually - laughed. You laughed at me!"

"Lavinia," this time he did smile.

"Oh, I love your smile, Stephen. Alright. I'll tell you. If your intentions are honorable, it is my considered opinion that she will entertain your suit."

He couldn't repress another smile.

"Now, I have just one more thing to ask you."

That is how Stephen Wenders came by Ruth-Ann Weathering's address.

# 16

The first time Stephen came to call on Ruth-Ann was a Saturday evening. They stood and talked outside the kitchen door.

"I suppose, Miss Weathering," he said, "that Lavinia's told you all about the crazy Wenders."

"What makes you say that?"

"Because I know Lavinia. How do you think I came upon where to find you? And if there's one thing Lavinia couldn't resist telling you - it's how crazy the Wenders are."

Ruth-Ann laughed. "Yes, she did say something about it."

"Just as I thought. I knew I would have to come to defend myself."

"Well?"

"Yes."

"Defend yourself."

"May we not walk about the premises?"

"Mr. Fleetwright does not take kindly to strange Colored men roaming about his property."

"Miss Weathering," smiled Stephen. "I must take exception to that statement. First of all, I am not strange. I am quite respectable. A gentleman's gentleman, conventional, you see. Not strange at all. Now, if you do not mean strange in that sense - the sense of being unusual - but that I am strange in that I am unknown to this household, then, again, I must object. I am known to a member of this household. You. Nor would I be roaming about his property. I would be escorting a very proper and beautiful young lady, one who happens to be in the homeowner's employ - and whose acquaintance I have made."

"Mmm," she said, smiling, impressed by his word play. "Well ... this once."

They looked at each other frequently as they walked. Each time their eyes met they both smiled.

"I ... uh. I really don't know why people think we're crazy," he said.

"Lavinia says it's because you're all too smart."

"Hmm. I don't know what she means, but ... uh, I think we are - or at least some of us are - a bit eccentric. My brother, Justis, for one, likes to invent things. He's always inventing something. Last month he said he completed work on an invention that will allow people to print whole newspapers just by taking photographs of what they want to print. I don't know the least thing about printing or photography so I haven't any idea whether his 'invention' has any merit. But Justis swears by it. Of course, he swears by most of his inventions.

"And, yes, there's my sister Persephone. She claims we - the Black Wenders - were descended from a West African royal family of what she calls the Fulani people. She has talked with a lot of our kinfolk, and as many people who lived in slavery times as possible. She went through the county records. And ... she has stolen various and sundry books and records from white folks. All of this she has put together ... and claims, on the basis of it, that we were lords and princes of a proud people in our native land possessed of a high civilization. She can talk to you about the Fulani clans and families for weeks - about what she calls their high places, and about how we got *here*. She puts on airs appropriate to the station from which she claims we came.

"But I think. I think the true reason people think we're crazy is because of Daddy, and what he has passed on ... to all of us."

They had reached the help's personal vegetable patches.

"Pretty gardens," said Stephen. "Which ones have you tended with your lovely hands?"

Ruth-Ann smiled. She said, "I can't tell you because I must be ware of the foxes, the little foxes, that spoil the vines; for our vines *have* tender grapes."

"Oh, Lord," said Stephen, "this child *do* read the bible."

They both laughed.

"Tell me," Ruth-Ann asked, "about what your Daddy passed on to all of you."

Stephen smiled. "I guess most people would say - it's craziness. Daddy. Daddy has always been a strong-willed man. Strong-willed. And there is one thing he has always said - he would be free. He would not abide to be under the heel of some white man. He would be free.

"His Mama and step-Daddy sharecropped. But he said, while he was still a boy, that he was going to strike out - he was going to get from under that. He would be free. He would raise himself up. He would be independent.

"He started doing odd-jobs as far back as he could remember. Hiding the money in an old bowl he buried. Used to work days and nights. When he was fifteen or sixteen, hired himself to work on an ocean ship. Stayed away three years. Came back with every penny he earned. That man - he went to Africa, places I never heard of - Freetown, and Leopoldville, and Durban. Went, he went - to China. A city they called Shanghai. I used to love to say that name: shang

... high. Shanghai. Went to London and Paris ... and a place in Brazil called Rio de Janeiro, said it meant River of January in Portugee. River of January. Said there were more Black people there than in Freetown, Leopoldville, and Durban put together. Said as far as he could see almost everybody in South America was Colored. That old man - went all over the world - and came back with every penny he ever made.

"Put it in his bowl. Hired himself out as a laborer. By the time he met Mama, he was in his middle twenties. Never had but one change of clothes at the same time in his whole life. He went to Claiborne Poole, a cousin of the White Wenders, and offered to pay him eight hundred dollars cash for fifty acres of cane-bottom land. When Claiborne gave him the deed, Daddy walked right over to Mama's stepfather, and asked him if he could marry his youngest daughter. One year later, after Daddy had built their cabin with his own hands, they were married.

"Daddy owns his own farm. Always has, ever since he was married. It's over three hundred acres now. We've always raised all our own food, chopped and split our own wood, built our own fences, cured our own hides. That man will not stand for the interference of white folk.

"He's always told us - stand up! Rise above this life they got marked out for Colored. Mark out your own life! So, I guess in that way, we're all crazy. Because I don't know anyone in our family who intends to stay down. We all intend to rise up and be independent - to be free! And we act like it. Folks call that crazy."

Ruth-Ann began to walk between the rows of plants. Stephen followed her. "Rising up," she said. "I like that."

She remembered what Mr. Turner had said about her. *If she finished high school, she could maybe go on to college. There's*

80

*nothing that a girl with her talent can't do.* She squeezed off the thought and turned her lips into a straight line.

She stopped, turned around and faced him. "May I call you Stephen?"

"Oh, yes," he said. "Please do."

"And you ... Stephen ... call me, Ruth-Ann."

"Thank you ... Ruth-Ann. Thank you, very much."

"I like that - rising up," she said. "But I don't really know what it means. I like the way it sounds. I like the way it *feels.* I just can't put a meaning to it."

For herself, she did not want to put a meaning to it. For her, that time was gone.

"I don't think I really know what it means for me either. I know what it means for Daddy. You can see what it means for him. In his life. In his work. How he lives and what he preaches to us. But I'm not Daddy, and I haven't figured out what it means for me.

"What I do know is what this world tells us - what life tells us - apart from my Daddy. It tells me I cannot dream. I cannot marry and take my wife on a holiday to stay at the best of hotels. I cannot build a future of bank accounts, and lands, and college matriculations for my children. Any night rider could tear such hopes to the ground in one night's savagery.

"But what am I to do *besides* dream, dream of another world? I don't know. My father has made me so that I cannot accept what is destined for me. But what that means I must do, I have not discovered.

"I've been to the North. A man can hold his head up. He doesn't have to step off the sidewalk for white folks. A man can vote. No riding in the jim-crow. No jim-crow. No special waiting rooms for colored. I've seen it. To some extent it's true - in some

81

places in the North. I don't know. It's true here, in the South, on my father's farm. On Lavinia's father's farm. They bow to no man, and they're not in the North."

"I guess, here, at least," she said, "it's better to be crazy."

They turned to walk back to the house. In the waning light without aid of eyes his hand sought and found hers. In all the world for the two of them there was only the joining of their hands. They did not see. They did not hear. As they walked on, their whole beings were concentrated in two linked hands.

\*

Ruth-Ann could not open her eyes in the mornings without the thought of Stephen Wenders entering her brain. She felt a chasm within her, a chasm that only he could fill by being with her always and ever. The thought that he might not return was too awful to entertain. She waited on each day as if it were a generation.

Saturdays. Saturdays became her own personal Gethsemane. If he were not to appear - if he were not to appear, surely she could not survive the night. Stephen came to see her Saturday evenings. He came each Sunday to the little country church she'd found in Baldwin. They went for long walks after church. Twice he wangled a row boat and they plied their way along the banks of the St. Johns.

With each moment Ruth-Ann felt she would never in her whole life stop falling into the infinite deep he had opened in her heart. Felt she could never stop falling, falling in love with this man.

# 17

Throughout the summer Stephen kept company with Ruth-Ann. He worked for a number of leading families throughout Duval County at various capacities while he looked for a position which met his own requirements.

Stephen had not married and had not asked any one to marry him because he had not met the right woman. He did not have his mind fixed on any particular characteristics in a woman. He simply knew he had not met the right one and he was willing to wait until he did.

He had no intention of remaining a bachelor permanently. He wanted very much to marry and have children, to be a family man. But he knew to start the family he wanted he would need a very special partner.

There was something about Ruth-Ann that struck him from the very moment he saw her at the picnic. He wanted to be around her. He found it hard to leave her. He wanted to get back to her as soon as he could. If he had articulated the feeling, he would have said he needed her.

That reality became all the more apparent when in late February, he was employed by a family which met his specifications and which was leaving for New England in mid-April. He realized then that he would be away from Ruth-Ann for up to six months and the prospect seemed terrifying. He had not yet faced the question of whether he wanted her to be his wife. She had turned sixteen while he had been seeing her. Stephen was twenty-eight. Yet - young as she was - he had met no one like her. He had met no one he wanted as much.

Happy as he was to have found the position he aspired to, he was disconsolate because it meant separating from Ruth-Ann. To compensate for his approaching privation, he saw her as frequently as he could for as long as he could. While they were together he let nothing enter his mind except the joy of being with her.

\*

When they were not together, however, things were not so straightforward. There was the question of her age. Twelve years younger than Stephen, *too* young?

To Stephen, it was not a simple question. He had lived long enough to know that people are not the same in the ways they mature. *If she matured early*, he thought, *and I matured late, twelve years - even at this time in our lives - might not be so great a distance. And with time that distance will narrow, as it becomes an increasingly smaller part of our lives.*

He knew, however, he was no late bloomer. His education had come late, but that was only his formal education. Indeed, it was his early maturation that enabled him to continue his education long after most young men had abandoned that path. No, he was not late maturing. He was early, even as Ruth-Ann was. Nor was he inexperienced. He was well seasoned in the ways of men and women, the ways of the world. Ruth-Ann was not. In that sense she was an innocent.

84

*What do I want with this girl? Was what I told Lavinia true, that my intentions are honorable?*

*I think so. Truly I do. I have no dearth of willing sweethearts. It is not out of desperation that I seek someone so young. Rather the contrary, I want her in spite of her age. Her youth is the sole impediment keeping me from throwing my heart at her feet. I do love his child. Should the difference between our ages be sufficient to set our love aside? For I truly believe that she loves me, too.*

The conviction that she did love him led to another quandary. *Her infatuation with me,* he thought, *might be because of my greater maturity, my greater ... age. She could become dependent on me because of these ... differences. She might be unable to see me realistically - until, until - with greater experience in this life, she perceives my feet of clay. Ah, that I could not bear, and it would be cruel, too cruel, to her.*

The question was unresolved for Stephen. It brought him such joy to be around her. But - oh - so young.

\*

When Stephen told Ruth-Ann his position was going to take him away from her in mid-April, she did not want to hear it and she told him never to say it again. She said if it were true, maybe they should stop seeing each other immediately so as not to waste each other's time since he was obviously toying with her affections.

"You told me - you told me - I didn't have to worry - you weren't going away to war. That may be true, Stephen. But you're still going away - you're still leaving *me!*"

85

She lowered her head. Her eyes filled with tears.

"Now. Now is the time for you to go, and not come back."

He begged, pleaded with her, not to say that, not to mean it. He had nothing but the highest regard for her and he entreated her not to send him away from her until the press of circumstance made his departure irresistible.

Why should I show such consideration to you, she asked, when you have shown none to me - to walk away and leave me, cold, cruel man.

He threw himself to his knees and swore he would not leave except that she knew - hadn't he explained it to her enough - how he was trying to better himself. Continuing to examine life in the North, and testing the ground there was an important part of how he was trying to do that. He would not be doing it at all - he would not - if it were not so important for the future, and now the future was more important than ever.

She dared not ask why.

She relented and said he could continue to see her but never to mention the date of his departure.

\*

As they walked from church one day in late March, hands linked, Ruth-Ann said,

"When do you leave for Massachusetts, what day?"

"You told me never to mention it, Ruth-Ann."

"Do you pay attention to everything I say? What is your last day heah?"

"Are you sure?"

86

"Is it a secret? Are you trying to keep it a secret from me?"

"No, but you -"

"Then, tell me. When are you leaving?"

April twelfth. We leave on the twelfth."

She snatched her hand away from his, she turned her back to him.

"How could you! How could you tell me that? How could you say those mean words to me?"

"Ruth-Ann."

He approached her.

He tried to face her.

She ran off from him down the road.

"Get away from me, Stephen Wenders," she called over her shoulder, "and never come near me again!"

He ran after her.

He caught her.

He held her hands.

"Please, please, forgive me," he pleaded. "I'm so sorry. Please, please, don't tell me not to see you again. I won't say - I won't say anything about it."

Her cheeks were tracked by tears. Her eyes were swollen. Her nose was red and dribbling.

"How can you hurt me this way," she demanded.

"I'm sorry. I'm sorry. Please, please, let me stay."

She walked on, saying nothing, but she didn't extricate her hand from his.

She didn't know what she was going to do.

She had never felt so bad in all her life.

Not even, she thought, not even when Calter died.

*How could that be? How could I be so selfish? What kind*

87

*of woman am I?*

*

Later, when Stephen did go north with his employers, Ruth-Ann became terrified. She learned what it was to have a broken heart.

She wrote Essie. She wrote Lavinia for understanding. What should she do? Should she cast him out of her life, close her mind to him? When he returned should she refuse to see him? Should she even write him? Was he using her for a plaything?

They did not know.

Essie wrote her saying that charity, "Beareth all things, believeth all things, hopeth all things, endureth all things."

Ruth-Ann read the letter and laughed to herself. *So does a fool.*

She cried bitterly.

One night from the middle of a deep sleep she came wide awake. She sat up.

I don't know how anything that hurts me so badly can possibly be good for me.

She put her hands on the beautifully carved wooden box that housed the letters he sent her and pushed it to the floor.

*

In Massachusetts, Stephen had a lot of time to think. His thoughts kept returning to Ruth-Ann. He wrote her. He wrote her

88

twice a week.

She did not answer.

He went nearly mad so that he could think of nothing else. He could barely do his work. Even the prized jug of hootch he had brought with him from the South could not console him. He wrote her seven days in a row. And seven more.

The next week he got his first letter from her.

He was swept into a delirium of joy.

After Ruth-Ann's first letter they corresponded.

He knew then he had to have this woman in his life permanently. He decided when he returned South he would court her seriously.

Through his letters he had already begun.

*Summer 1917*

# 18

Weathering kin came to the wedding by the wagon-load. They came in all their ages and sizes, men and women, boys and girls. They came in their many colors and physical types, hair textures and facial features. Ruth-Ann was a family favorite. They came to celebrate.

From way across the other side of Jacksonville, the Wenders came. They came riding in two wagons to meet their Stephen's bride. They, too, came laughing and smiling, filled with elation for the occasion. The proud patriarch drove their leading wagon. They were all tall - tall and beautiful and crazy. On first blush they were taken with Ruth-Ann and without hesitation, indeed, with wild enthusiasm, welcomed her as one of their strange, fierce clan.

\*

Stephen and Ruth Ann's first home as Mr. and Mrs. Wenders, was Stephen's room at the Northrups', where he worked. It was a small room above the garage. They both knew it was not suitable for two people other than for a honey moon. Stephen's job required him to be away from Jacksonville six months out of the year. Now that they were married, pledged always to come back to one another, the separation would be bearable. Ruth-Ann had her job with the Fleetwrights. She would be there while Stephen was gone. But they needed a place of their own when he returned from the North.

On a whim, one day after he'd dropped Mr. Northrup at the railroad station for a business trip, Stephen took a meandering route home. When he picked up Ruth-Ann that evening, he was brimming over with liveliness.

He ran to her almost before she could get out of the back door.

"Oh, girl, wait till you see what I found."

She knew right away he was talking about a place and she started laughing.

"Tell me about it, Stephen," she cried.

As they hurried down the driveway to the car, he started to, but then thought better of it.

"No," he said. "I want you to see it for yourself. I want your own eyes to tell you about it before I say a word."

"Tonight?"

He burst out laughing.

"Girl, it's dark. What do you think you're going to see in the middle of the night?"

"When, then?"

They reached the car and Stephen saw Ruth-Ann in. He walked around to his side. As he opened his door, she was saying,

"When, then, Stephen, when can I see it?"

He sat down in the car and closed his door. He put both hands on the steering wheel and faced the windshield. With a little nod his sober face broke into a smile and he turned to look at her.

"What about tomorrow," he said. "We get up early and I take you by there on the way to work. It's just a hop skip and a jump from where we're sitting right now."

She broke out into a wild shower of laughter. She reached over and hugged him.

# 19

The sun had not cleared the horizon as they turned onto the narrow bayside road, but there was enough light to see. *Trees*, thought Ruth-Ann. *There's a woods here.* Stephen drove slowly to keep the car from bouncing on the pot-holed road.

"Anybody live out heah," she asked, turning to her husband.

"Heh, heh, heh," he laughed, turning to look at her, "one of the best things about this place is that I'm going to have you all to myself." He made his eyes go big and released a shriek.

"Stephen, don't you scare me with your Wenders craziness."

She turned away from him and looked out through the windshield. The road seemed to stretch ahead of them for a long, long way.

"I thought you said this was close to the Fleetwrights'," she said.

"Compared to the Northrups,' it is," he said. "Couldn't be more than a mile and a half."

"No, a mile and a half's not bad, Stephen Wenders, but I don't see any house - and this is a long, long, old road."

"I'm in your way," he said. He drove a little further, then pulled over to the far right-hand side of the road. He reached over, put his arm around her shoulder, and brought her close to him. "Now, look over there," he said, pointing at a sharp angle to his right.

She saw then that the bay did not come right up to the road. A spit of land ran along the bay side of it. About a hundred yards further a little house stood on a raised pitch of ground. There was sand around it and high saw-grasses. As she looked, the sun started coming up directly behind the house. The front of the structure was dark, in shadow, but there were rays of light, copper and amber radiating all around it. The dwelling gleamed like a jewel, the vast water lying serene behind it.

"Oh, beautiful," she said in a small voice. She stared.

She turned to her husband.

"Can it truly be ours, Stephen?"

"I just wanted to get you over here to see the outside this morning," he said. "I've got t'get you back to work - and get over to the Northrups.' I looked at the inside yesterday and I think you'll like it. It's been kept up nice. Nobody's lived in it for over a year. I talked to the man in Baldwin and he said he'd let us rent it for less than half the price we've been hearing for other places - places that couldn't hold a candle to this one."

She squeezed his arm and pushed her head into his shoulder. "When can we get it?"

"Let's not rush," he said. "I want you to see the house up close, to go inside and look around. See what you think. The man said he wouldn't have any trouble holding it for us. He wants to make sure when he gets a tenant, he gets a good one."

She held tightly to his arm. She smiled.

# 20

*Somebody been in my woods.*

The old man scratched in his long, matted beard. He no longer thought much about the crabs and lice in it. He just scratched when he itched. A few flies buzzed around him. His body emitted a pungence that attracted them. He paid them no attention. He knelt down to examine the bent grass, the marks on the thick matt of needles and leaves on the forest floor.

He grinned. He stood up.

*No. Not somebody. Somebody's dog.*

*One o` them two nigga families what lives on the bayside road. Prob'ly lettin` one o` they mangey hounds run loose t` keep from feedin` it. He, he, he, he. Well, that's they choice. Won't have t` feed it no mo!* He stretched.

*I got t` get me somethin` t` take care o` this ol` hound dog,* he thought.

He went to his house by following a dry creek bed. He went inside only long enough to pick up a long hunting rifle and some ammunition. He wasted no time but followed the creek bed back to where he'd read the dog signs.

He studied the area carefully. Then he began to track the animal.

About an hour and a half later he saw the dog ahead of him. It was lying down in deep shade. The old man eased himself down on his hands and knees. He slithered along through the underbrush, keeping broad trees between himself and his target. He got down wind, then came closer, carefully, without sound.

He stopped about seventy feet off and studied the animal.

Big.

*Got some bloodhound in him. Mastiff, too. Somethin` else I can't tell.*

The man moved very slowly, a hunter's moves.

He got into a kneeling position. He brought the rifle up to his shoulder. He took a long aim. He squeezed the trigger smoothly.

The gun roared and kicked.

The dog slumped, a bullet in his brain.

The man stood up, grinning ear to ear.

*I got meat for two weeks.*

# 21

He stepped out of the woods onto the road. He crossed it and the spit of sand leading to the house. He walked all around the house, peering into the windows. He examined the ground. He scratched at his ribs. He walked onto the porch and tried the door. It was locked. He laughed. He walked down from the porch, past the house and into the water. It felt good on him. He laid down and rolled around in it. At last he stood and walked out.

He shook himself like a dog. Water went flying out from all over him, especially from his long, matted hair and beard.

He glanced at the house and the tracks in the sand. He licked his cracked and bleeding lips. He loved the salty taste.

He loved that old Foley place, out on a stretch of sand and grass all by itself. Some tasty nigger-wench was always settin' up in there for housekeeping. And he got them. He got them all. Every now and then the place would stand empty. People afraid to rent it. But after awhile they forgot or didn't know about it and somebody delicious moved in. It were as if the house was a cook pot setting on a fire, all ready for the choicest morsel to be dropped in, just for Effraim.

He chuckled to himself. There was nothin' like a young Colored girl. They had the tastiest meat ever put around a bone. He'd been fourteen years old in 1859. He'd never been with a female. His father, who owned forests and cane fields and orchards for miles around, and all the slaves needed to work them, had wanted him broken into manhood. So he'd brought him to the slave pens.

He'd had his pick, any wench he wanted. He'd picked one out with that sunny brown color, smooth, soft skin, much developed female parts all around. His father had made her man leave the cabin and Effraim had her there on her pallet. He'd never known anything like it. Lying there with her had awakened something in him he'd never imagined was there. He'd lain with her all night - and couldn't leave the next day - and wouldn't leave the day after that. He'd stayed with her three days and three nights before his father dragged him on away from there. He would have stayed there forever if he could. He never got it out of his system. In fact, it got worse. Like a disease. He burned with it. Every spare minute he could find he was down in those slave pens. Fornicating.

The girl he'd spent that first night with, Fenny, had borne him his first child, a boy they'd named Harry. She bore him two girls after that, Rose and Neena. Her man got so he would just leave whenever he saw Effraim coming. Couldn't call him her husband. Niggers weren't allowed to marry. Just the man she lived with. She'd had a couple pickaninnies by that man before Effraim got his hands on her. Fenny. Yes, that was his first nigger-wench.

Effraim no longer knew how many children he'd had by how many women. He didn't care. But he remembered those first three, and he remembered how good it was getting them. A father by the time he was fifteen. The damn war came and ruined everything. Of course, they'd kept their slaves right up to the very end of the war, and he'd just about lived in the slave pens all through it. Women were everywhere and all his. He couldn't get over the joy, the excitement of that feeling. That he was always surrounded by women he could have every one of. That knowledge alone kept him in a permanent state of sexual arousal.

They said he had the balls and the member of a billy goat.

He didn't know. He just knew he could do it all day and all night without getting tired and the longer he did it the better it got to him. When he wore out one bitch he'd just move on to the next. He never got enough. But the Yankees had won the damn war. That meant he couldn't command it when he wanted it, he had to find ways to take it, to get it the best way he could.

Most of his father's wealth was in slaves, so when the war freed them, he lost almost all of his capital. He had plenty land, though, and cattle, pigs, chickens, and horses. He was not a poor man by a long shot. He was simply no longer as rich as a king. He had a house in town and a country house. Except now he had to pay the help. He didn't have to pay them all, though. He took to having the freed niggers take on shares with him early-on, before others caught on to it. Then, after reconstruction was over, he got most of his labor, free, from the peonage. That kept Efraim well supplied with nigger women. He could take the share croppers' women when he got good and ready - their daughters and their wives. White men had to string up a few of the Colored men before they got a proper understanding of the way things were. Then, with the peonage - those women belonged to them, just the same as slaves. The only thing, there weren't as many. But it was alright.

Effraim had always liked adventure, though, so he figured out other ways to satisfy his tastes as well. Hell, he was a young stallion. He thrived on excitement. His best trick was hiding out in the evening, early dark, by the outhouses. Most people liked to use the outhouse before they went to bed. That way they could usually sleep through the night without having to relieve themselves. Many people used a slop bucket if they had to get up during the night. They'd empty it in the morning. But most people preferred not to have to use it. They tried to clean themselves out before retiring.

98

Effraim would pick an outhouse used by several likely gals. In the dark, in the deepest shadows, he'd hide where he was nearly invisible. Either they'd bring a light - a candle or lantern - or there'd be enough moonlight for him to tell who the women were. He'd watch them, and he'd take his pick - the one he wanted most of all. Then he'd jump her with her pants down. She didn't have a chance.

A lot of those girls were strong. But Effraim had always been a big, strong thing, and he had the advantage. He got them by surprise with a skirt, a dress, or pantaloons down by their ankles. Sometimes the fight was rough. But he always got his way with them, and over the years built up a lot of experience about just what to do. He laughed at the memory of it, rolling and kicking in the dirt, the feeling of sticks and grass against the body, the smell of fear - hers and his.

He grunted.

Those thoughts kept him going - even now. He'd never had a taste for white women. With their skin either so pale you could see the blue veins showing through or reddened by the sun, looking like something that had been boiled in hot water, their skin all rough. No, they never did a thing for him. He didn't like their skinny lips and their stringy hair. He detested their flat asses and hairy legs. Give him colored every time.

He never thought about marriage. Why should he? He'd be saddled with some white woman and whatever brats they'd make. She'd try to spend his money and run his life. No thanks. He didn't need that. He could have as many women as he could take - dark, sweet women, too. And, hell, he'd made enough babies to populate a village and didn't have to be worried about raising them. Hell, he'd *owned* three of his own children.

Effraim was pleased with himself. He'd lived a good life.

After his father's death he and his brothers and sisters had sold off most of the land. Their mother had died when he was ten. Effraim made a passel of money from the land sales. He didn't have to work. He'd kept the six square miles of woodland he lived in. He'd lived there now for twenty-five years. The house he occupied used to be the house of his father's head timberman and his family. Both the house and the position had been vacant ten years before Effraim moved in. He'd fixed it up to his liking. He'd always been handy and he relished the physical work.

The house was deep in the heart of his woods. Few people knew it was there. He never came to it or went from it in ways that would leave a trail. He approached and departed from it in different ways, so that no single way got worn down. He learned how to walk in stream beds, gulleys, and on beds of dead leaves and pine needles. He learned to traverse his forest in all the ways that left no hint of his coming or going. He patrolled the boundaries of his wilderness to spot any animal trails which might open it up to human trespassers. He covered them with logs and bushes and dead branches to prevent points of access, so that it would appear uninhabited and inaccessible. He loved hiding and peeking out to see what he could see, but mostly he loved observing the young colored girls.

Once he found one to his liking, he studied her. He learned everything about her he could, whether she had a regular schedule, her times of arrival and departure, her pace, her alertness, whether she was ever accompanied. If he could watch her dwelling, he found out who lived with her, whether she had visitors. He learned what time she went to bed and when she got up, the work she did around the house. He used all the information he had to plot her abduction.

He always took a long time. He was meticulous. He didn't like surprises. He wanted absolute certainty. He also enjoyed the build-up. The teasing, the prospect of eventually having her worked him up. She became an obsession with him, and he lived for the plotting, the reconnaissance, the watching.

A glimpse of her caused his throat to dry out and his mouth to salivate. His head throbbed. His heart vaulted in his chest. His penis swelled so that it hurt him, rigid and heavy in his pants.

He drew out the waiting. The expectation was agonizingly sweet. When the event finally came it crowned a long and deeply felt experience, crowned it with glory.

Over the years Effraim had taken at least a score of girls on this very road, some more than once. He dragged them off the road and into the woods and had them. He had to beat some savagely before he could possess them. He tried to beat them in the stomach and groin or on the back of the head. He did not like to kiss bloody mouths and faces. He could subdue some by getting them in a painful hold or twisting their arms or legs or fingers. Occasionally, he had to break a finger, a hand, or arm. He preferred not to bruise and batter them, so that he got all the sweetness.

He took the very best girls off to his house. He tied them up and ravished them at will for months. He made them promise not to tell about his house, or he would visit terrible retribution on them and their families. They were to say they ran off with some young buck for a few months - a common enough behavior - which made it believable.

He hadn't taken many girls off the road recently, only two in the past four years. Those who lived in the area were wise to him. He laughed. He'd caught too many.

Sometimes, when the anticipation was especially exciting, Effraim exposed himself to his victim a few days before he finally snatched her. That got him worked up to a fever-pitch. He showed her what she was about to get. The blood pounded through his system like drum beats. She was shocked - and terrified - violence and electricity charged the air.

When he exposed himself beforehand, he put into her mind exactly what she had coming. She would anticipate it as he did, but she would anticipate it with terror. When at last he stepped out of the woods to grab her, she knew both the horror and the terrible finality of it. Usually, by then her fright had so incapacitated her that she couldn't resist him. He took her into the woods, and into his sequestered retreat, without a struggle.

He didn't do that often. It was too risky. It alerted her. But it also prepared the way for the ultimate, for the most ravishing of his conquests, those young, tender bodies who would transport him across time to the slave pens and his first nights with Fenny.

# 22

When Ruth-Ann and Stephen moved in they didn't say much. They walked around in the house, sat down, held hands. They went outside and walked in the sand, they kept turning to look back at the house, then came inside. Darkness found them holding hands and looking out of the window. Silent. Listening to the water.

She loved the freedom the place gave her. There was not another house on the road for a mile in either direction. On the other side lay the dense and unbroken woods. A whole day could go by when not a single person passed by. That meant Freedom to Ruth-Ann. She could run around the house. She could laugh and shout without worrying about annoying anybody. She could sing - inside the house and out. She and Stephen could play and tussle in the middle of the night and she could cry out in her passion without fear of offending a soul. It was a complete release from her job where she always had to be proper, in perfect control, where she was continually under the eyes of others.

Their neighbors - a mile between each house - were colored, so Ruth-Ann figured she would know them in time. They seemed friendly, smiling. They waved and hollered greetings whenever they saw her. But there was no rush. She and Stephen needed time for each other. The neighbors said they were glad to see somebody living in the house. They asked Stephen if he'd seen the old man but he didn't know who they were talking about.

Rather than have Stephen drive her to and from work, Ruth-Ann preferred to walk, especially since they lived so near the

Fleetwright's. Even when it rained she didn't mind. She covered up, wore rubber boots, and walked right on through the mud and water. If the mud got too deep, she walked in the grass at the side of the road.

The transitions she went through twice a day intrigued her. On the way to work she saw the change as soon as she got onto the main avenue. White people lived there. She passed two general stores, a dentist's office, and a lawyer's office. A block away she saw the white school. She walked by prosperous-appearing houses, close together, with fences and neat yards. All the streets were paved. There were even street lamps.

The Fleetwrights' house was the biggest one she came to, but there were many where yardmen and gardeners raked and trimmed and dug and planted. It was too early in the morning for her to see nurse-maids in the yards with children. Horse drawn wagons and carriages passed her as well as automobiles and trucks.

On the way home, the transition was just as complete. It began when she reached her own road. The road itself was the be-speaker of change. It was rutted and full of pot-holes. Often puddles adorned it. Many were long, wide, and deep. Some spanned the whole drive, even when it had not rained in a week or two. When there had been no rain for a long time, the surface was dry and dusty. The breaks in it were more like canyons and gullies than potholes. In some places, weeds - even in the dry times - grew in the middle of the thoroughfare.

The way home also differed from what she left behind because it was empty. On the left ran the unbroken woods - dark and tall. Across from them, only a narrow strip of land lay between the road and the bay. In the whole walk after the transition began, she passed only two houses, each small and run down, inhabited by other

Colored folk. No whites. But the Colored people always had a neighborly greeting for her, unlike the whites on the main street who seemed never to see her.

Warm as her widely spaced neighbors were, for some reason she could not define, when Ruth-Ann turned onto her little road, when she looked down its long straight path, so devoid of human habitation, she felt a swoop of panic. It was not unfamiliar. She'd experienced it hundreds of times when she saw ahead of her the mile-long stretch of Nightmare's fence. Every time she turned onto her new road, terror grabbed her. It only lasted an instant, but it never failed to appear. After it passed, she became happier with each step, so glad to be nearing her own little cottage.

*

From the very first day the girl appeared, Effraim Patterson rejoiced in the sight of her. He had seen her when her husband brought her to look at the old Foley place. They'd only stayed a hot minute, parked on the road across from the house, but that was long enough for him to know he liked her - wanted her. After that, every time she went by, he had his eyes on her. He often went to the Foley place to sniff around after her when no one was there. She was just the kind he liked. Golden-brown color. Full bodied. Young. Sweet. Now this tender dumpling was waiting for him to pluck her.

He watched her all the time. He made his plans, more careful than ever, and he watched her. His seed was old, but she made it boil inside him. He licked his lips. Pretty soon this old pot's goin` ta boil right over, honey. It's goin` ` ta boil over inside o` you.

# 23

Exactly when the dreams returned, Ruth-Ann did not know. With the first ones, Stephen gentled her, the dreams left, and she settled into peaceful sleep. She did not remember them. The horrible dreams she'd had since her encounter with Nightmare had stopped the Fourth of July she'd met Stephen. But sometime after they moved into their little home, they returned. At first because of Stephen's attentiveness, she hadn't realized she was having them. But gradually, they became more intense. Stephen had to awaken her to free her from them. When she came screaming into consciousness, they lived on in her mind.

He wanted to know what was wrong. She told him the dreams were back, that she'd had them as a child. Now, they'd returned, not every night. For a long time she did not even have them weekly. But in time she had them two, finally three times a week. She started fearing sleep because she never knew when they might come. Sometimes they came three nights in a row. Other times they were spaced. She never knew.

\*

Stephen was thinking about when he'd be going back North again. April. It would be in April, when he would leave, without Ruth-Ann. He didn't like the feel of that. They were married. They should be together.

Going North for half the year had become a habit for him.

Just as it had for the various families for whom he'd worked. It was a pattern built into his life while he was a single man. He didn't want to keep that pattern as a husband.

He knew men, married men, who separated from their wives and families every year. There were even married women who worked in service who were with their families half a year. That was no way to be. He even knew people, married people, who lived apart all the time. The one working up North - usually it was the man, but sometimes it was the woman - sent money back every month, sometimes every week. They only got to see each other on short visits. Sometimes a whole year - and even more - might go by, without seeing each other. *I don't see much point in that kind of marriage,* thought Stephen. *We didn't get married to live like that. But what am I going to do? Come April, I'll have to go North. And leave Ruth-Ann right here, in our little house. It's pretty enough. And it's safe enough. Nobody out here to bother her. But I expect it will be lonely. She's never lived by herself. Maybe ... I know she's the oldest ... but maybe she could get one of her sisters to stay out here with her, off and on.*

Every day confirmed for him that getting married had been the right thing for them to do. In his whole life he had never felt so good, so right. She was the companion for him, his life's companion. But ... come April, things were going to change. He didn't like the idea of his wife's being lonely.

*

Essie was the first one from Jacksonville to come see them at the cottage.

107

Ruth-Ann was beside herself with excitement. She showed off her handiwork - curtains, bedspreads, doilies. She took Essie outside to walk on the sand, to look at the house from different angles, and to marvel at the wide view of the bay.

They sat on a point of sand where the water all curdled at its edges washed up close to their feet then drew back sighing.

Essie's eyes were wide.

"I can see married-life agrees with you," she said. She laughed, song-like, the wind carrying it out over the water.

When Stephen came home, the three of them sat together and talked long into the darkness.

*

Their second visitor was Lavinia. One of her brothers brought her in a horse-driven carriage. He dropped her off and said he'd be back for her after suppertime.

She was as wild and flamboyant as ever. She stepped out of the carriage with her mouth running. Ruth-Ann took one look at her and burst out laughing. She ran to Lavinia, her arms wide-open.

"Mmmm - girl, don't you look somethin'," said Lavinia, even as Ruth-Ann ran to her. "Married and everything - ooh, child, I hope you aren't pregnant."

They hugged.

Lavinia introduced Ruth-Ann to her brother, then he was off.

Ruth-Ann took her friend's hand.

"Girl, I thought we lived out in the country," said Lavinia as they walked up to the house. "But y'all live near 'bout in the natural wilderness.

"My, don't you know those woods on the other side of the road - there's not a break in them. Baxter and I both looked the whole while we came along there - looked hard, too, and not a break did we see - wilderness girl, wilderness!

"We saw, though, it is not without its residents."

"Residents? What are you talking about, Lavinia?"

"We saw some old pale face peeking through the trees - eyes locked right on me! Looked like they wanted to eat me up. Who is that?"

"Lavinia, I don't know what you're talking about. I walk past those woods everyday, going a good deal slower than you were in your carriage, and I have never seen anyone."

"Alright, Mrs. Wenders," Lavinia shrieked at her use of the title. *"Mrs. Wenders.* You can say what you like, but I know what I saw. I couldn't see it clearly enough to tell whether it was old or young, man or woman. It was pale alright, though. That was a white face I saw looking at me - unless it was an albino. And, of course, it must have been a man. No woman would have been looking at me like that."

"Lavinia, you always think somebody's after your britches."

Lavinia burst out laughing. "That's because they are. Come on girl, show me your house, and tell me what married life is like."

They laughed and played the whole day.

Lavinia was full of farm stories and she made Ruth-Ann take her wading out into the bay and digging for clams, and fishing. They recited poetry. Ruth-Ann cooked, they ate and cleaned the dishes together. Ruth-Ann wanted to know if Lavinia had any beaus.

"Oh, girl, they're all after me," said Lavinia. "But I can't be studdin` about any of those boys. I'm having too much fun living at home and having my Daddy take care of me. Now which one of

109

those boys can treat me that well?  I'll tell you - narry a one!  No, child.  I'm not about to leave this good thing."

They laughed.  When Baxter came back for Lavinia and drove off with her, Ruth-Ann stood in the road and watched them go, water standing in her eyes.

*

Stephen wanted to hear all about Lavinia's visit.  Ruth-Ann told him and got happy all over again.  Lavinia was so full of life. Stephen laughed.  He knew Lavinia almost as well as Ruth-Ann did.

"Next time she's got to stay long enough for me to see her, too," he said.

Ruth-Ann laughed.  "Yes, won't the three of us have a time?"

She didn't mention the pale face.  A pale face - not definitely old or young, male or female - was not much to go on.  It could have been a possum.  Ruth-Ann laughed to herself.  Yes.  Maybe that's what it was.  A possum.

Her eyes twinkled.

"What you laughin' at, girl?"

"Layos to fetch meddlers," she said.

"I'll show you some meddlin'," he said, chasing her into the bedroom.

Their passion was long and sweet, easing them into sleep.

*

Out of the woods with his great, filthy, reeking self, he came. He surveyed the road up and down.  No one.  He looked out onto the bay.  Not a boat in sight.  He grinned.  He looked down, then,

110

studying the road's surface.

*Aha. There.*

He put his great bare foot forward. He paid no attention to his splayed, grimy toes. He put his huge foot directly onto the footprint.

*Heh, heh, heh, heh. Little feet.*

He put one foot down after the other, in mincing steps, for about sixty feet.

He stopped.

*Little thing*, he thought.

He scratched the wildly twisted hair on the top of his head.

He studied the bare footprints as they went off in the dust.

He looked all around him again. Then he blended back into the trees.

# 24

The sand around the cottage was perfect for digging. When Ruth-Ann had been a girl - she thought of herself before she was married as a girl - now she was a woman, when she had been a girl living at home with her family, she had loved to dig in the sand. She bounced down the steps to it. It was warm on her bare feet. She loved that feeling. The day was warm, but not hot. A freshening breeze blew off the water. She inhaled deeply. She loved the smell of the air off the sea. She walked leisurely along the beach.

*I know I'm a grown woman*, she thought, *but I can indulge myself for a few minutes. I'm not **old**. I'll just plop myself down on the sand and dig - with my hands - as I did when I was a child - which wasn't that long ago.*

She laughed at herself.

She kept walking.

She looked all around.

As usual, there was no one in sight. Not even a boat on the bay. She was the sole human being for at least a mile in every direction.

She giggled. *Who would know?*

With one last glance about her, she dropped to the sand, on her butt. She drew her skirt up just past her knees and spread her legs out to the side. Slowly, savoring every sensation, she began to slip both hands into the warm sand in the space between her parted legs. She bent over so that her head was directly above her hands, now out of sight, the lower part of her forearms immersed in the fine particles.

In easy, smooth motions she scooped the sand up and deposited it in a pile at her feet. *I'm only going to do this for a few minutes,* she thought. But as she dug, it was as if she were transported back to the carefree days of her childhood. No job. No mister and mistress to approve her. No rent. No bills to pay. No food to buy. Just the joy of life and the satisfaction of her whims. She laughed.

The hole got deeper and the pile higher. She had to shift her position.

She was on her knees now, scooping furiously.

Sweat streamed down her brow. She wiped her forehead and got sand in her eyebrows. Perspiration stuck her dress to her body.

The breeze seemed to have slacked off.

The hole was getting too deep for her to be able to reach the bottom from the kneeling position. She was going to have to widen it so she could get down into it. She would stop piling the sand in one place. She would make a ring of it around the hole.

She wasn't sure. She was too far down in the hole and the mounds around its edge were too high, but she thought the sun was appreciably lower in the sky. Lord, the last thing she wanted was to have Stephen come home and find her in this chasm. She laughed. She knew she would have to stop in a few minutes. It was such hot work.

Night had come. She could not see. Above her the sky was too dark.

She screamed.

The squirming wriggling thing flopped out of her hands.
Hoppy-Toad.
She heard it hit the bottom of the damp hole.
She ran.
She could not see where she was going, but she ran.
She heard it hopping behind her.
She screamed.
She must have crossed the road.
Even in the dark she could sense the massive wall of trees ahead of her.
*"Stephen!"*
She heard it behind her.
She looked over her shoulder.
Tall.
Black.
Mane in the wind.
He filled the sky.
She turned back around screaming, screaming, screaming.
She fell down.
She heard behind her an instant of sound, then nothing.
An instant of sound.
She knew if she screamed loudly enough she would tear her throat out.
*"Darling, darling, please, please, it's alright."*
Her eyes bolted open.
Stephen was looking down at her. His face was tight with worry.
"Oh, Stephen, it's you, it's you, it's you."
She clung to him, her strong hands gripping his hard muscles, her nails tearing into his skin.

114

She hung on for life.

*

He liked to come to the edge of the woods near the house on the spit. That way he could hear her. He could hear her laughing and talking. He loved the sound of her voice. The laughing so full of merriment and vivacity. The talking so melodious and intimate. It made his heart ache.

He heard the singing, the melody lilting across the road to him. He could imagine it went the other direction, too, over the bay.

When she came out of the house she moved with the freedom of a wild thing. She was a joy to behold.

At any time, in the dark of night, early in the mornings, or even in the afternoon he might hear her moans and shouts of passion. He waited for those. He closed his eyes to those. As if they were being said into his own ears. As if they were in response to his ardor. Sometimes they made him reach down into his pants where he had grown long, and thick, and hard. He held on and squeezed, sometimes making his own garbling noises, until the relief came shooting out of him. Those times he forgot all about the crabs itching him down there.

He heard the other screams deep in the night, too.

They were not screams of love.

He had heard screams like that before.

He had caused them.

# 25

"I don't know what I'm going to do when you go away, Stephen. Please don't be gone too long."

Stephen didn't want to hear those words. He'd been pondering over them long and hard, but he didn't want to hear them. He'd come to no conclusion and he didn't want his inadequacy exposed. He didn't want to reveal his own concern. She didn't need to be carrying two sets of worries. He tried to distract her.

"Ruth-Ann, you know how long I'll be."

"I don't know what I'm going to do."

"You'll be fine. You are very good at taking care of yourself - even the spring chicken that you are." He wasn't really worried about her taking care of herself. She was an immensely capable young woman, lord, had he discovered that. No, she could take care of herself and somebody else, too. He didn't want her to be lonely. He didn't want them to be apart.

"Don't call me a spring chicken. I'm a grown woman!"

He bent over laughing. "I'm sorry. I'm sorry. I know you're a fully grown woman, all of seventeen years. Yes, I do. But what's all this talk about you don't know what you're going to do?"

"I don't mean that. I don't mean I can't take care of myself. I mean you. I need you. I don't know what I'm going to do without you."

That's exactly what he felt. *Exactly*. "This time we'll write," he said.

She smiled. "Yes, this time we'll write. *I'll write*."

"Good, that's a relief," he said.

116

"We'll write," he repeated, "and the next thing you know, I'll be home again."

"It's lonely out heah," she said.

Stephen winced. She had hit on it. That was what bothered him the most. *She would be alone. Very alone. Nobody ever came out this way, so no one should bother her. But it wasn't good. A woman alone out here. It was different with the two of them, then it was private. But with just her - she **would** be alone. Not good. Maybe she could get somebody to come stay with her, one of her sisters, or Essie, Lavinia. Lavinia would be perfect. Somebody. Maybe we can do that.*

"Who's going to wake me up when I have nightmares, Stephen?"

He held her tight. *Yes. That was something nobody else could replace.*

After a while he said, "Let's hope you don't have anymore."

"I always have them," she said into his chest. "Not every night. But they always come back."

He kissed her on the cheek. *She was right.*

She held onto him tightly.

"I need you, too," he said. "But we'll get through this. We'll get through this and in a little while we'll build a new life for ourselves." He kissed her forehead. "You are my Rose of Sharon and my Lily of the Valley. We are going to put all this out of our minds and enjoy the time we have left. Every minute."

She hugged him hard. "Every minute," she said.

He knew they could not just muddle through this. They had to *think* a way out of it. He kissed the back of her hand.

# 26

The day was so hot and oppressive that for the first time Ruth-Ann was gladdened by the dark and foreboding forest that sheered off the sky to her left when she turned onto her road. But while she left the sun's direct glare, heat did not leave her. Her skin, damp with perspiration, adhered to the light fabric of her dress. With each step, the hot, humid fog enveloping her body became less bearable. The insects hovering about her irritated her to distraction, but she could not summon the energy to shoo them away. She couldn't remember an early spring that had been so hot. It's like mid-summer, she thought.

"Miz Wenders. Yahoo! Miz Wenders!"

The friendly voice cut through the torpor.

Ruth-Ann looked for its source.

There, back from the road, standing on her porch, waving at her was Mrs. Wabash.

"Howdy, Mrs. Wabash!"

"Miz Wenders! Come on heah out `n dat `midity an` git yosef a glass o` lemonade fo` you continues down de road in dis-heah heat."

Ruth-Ann stopped. It seemed a reasonable suggestion. She smiled.

"Thank you, Ma'am," she said and headed for the Wabash porch.

When she got to the front porch, Mrs. Wabash directed her into the front room.

"Have a seat, have a seat," said Mrs. Wabash. "I'm gointer de back t'po' you a jar o' lemonade. It's good. I jest made it, chile. I be right back."

"Thank you, Mrs. Wabash."

Ruth-Ann sank into the chair. She could feel the wicker pressing into her wet skin through the dress. She didn't care. She sat still in the chair and didn't move.

"I say," said Mrs. Wabash, walking back into the living room with a big jar full of lemonade, "you stays too long out in dat sun today an' you gon' cook yosef to a frazzle."

She handed Ruth-Ann the jar.

"Thank you, Ma'am."

She took the container and drew a long, deep swallow.

"Ah," she said at last. "That hits the spot."

Mrs. Wabash sat down.

"I thought so. I watched fo' you. You usually goes by 'bout dis time an' I couldn't see you trudgin' down all de way t' yo' place in dis heah heat widout a rest stop."

Ruth-Ann laughed. "Well, I'm surely glad you did. Yes, I am."

"Somebody else be watchin' fo' you, too, Miz Wenders. You got t' mine' yo' p's and q's on dis-heah ol' road."

"Ma'am?"

"I's talkin' 'bout ol' Pattison."

"I'm sorry, Mrs. Wabash. I don't know who that is."

"You don't know 'bout Pattison? My lordy, why dat explain it den."

Ruth-Ann took another sip of lemonade and gave Mrs. Wabash a bewildered look.

"I mean it explain why y'all moved inter dat house on de spit.

119

`Cose it nevuh entered nobody's head you didn't know `bout Pattison. We thought evybody knowed ` bout Pattison. But y'all ain't from ovuh dis way. I guess you ain't heered of him ovuh deah in dem parts you's from."

Ruth-Ann shook her head. "No, Ma'am."

"Well, do-tell. Who would of knowed it? Cause Pattison is sho` well knowed in dese parts. Pattison is de ol` white man what live in de woods."

"He's the old man," asked Ruth-Ann.

"Yes'm."

*The old man. Lavinia's face. Now it had age and gender to it. And a man. Not a possum.*

She was suddenly frightened.

"I didn't know anybody lived in the woods."

"Well. He do. Calls him ol` Effy Pattison. A white man. Lived dere for `bout near long as any somebody kin dismember. Dey say - cose I ain't never seed it an` don't know nobody what have, but dey say he got a house some'ere's yonder back in dem woods."

"Mrs. Wabash, I go by those woods every day and I have never seen anybody. I have never seen even a path or a trail."

Ruth-Ann did not want to believe what her neighbor was telling her. Soon she would be living alone in her house.

"Dat's right. It ain't no path or trail what I knows of. An if ol` Effy don't want you t` see him, you sho` ain't go` see him, neither. But he dere alright. I seen him de udder day."

Ruth-Ann's eyes widened, but she didn't say anything. She took another drink of lemonade.

"What does he do?"

"Uh huh," said Mrs. Wabash. "Dat's what got hissef so

120

knowed in dese heah parts. What he do. He grabs hissef cullud girls. Dat's what he do. He drags'em back in dem woods an` have his way wid ` em. Likes `em young an` sweet, too. `Bout yo` age."

Ruth-Ann's mouth dropped open. She felt goose bumps on her skin. The day was just as hot but she felt goose bumps on her skin. She felt chill.

"But I have never seen anybody."

"Dat's good. 'Cause you ain't gwineter see him but once or twice befo` he gits you."

"Gets me?"

"Well, Miz Wenders, he might not will git you. But I's gwineter tell you dis-heah. He gwinter try."

Ruth-Ann stared at Mrs. Wabash in disbelief. Did she know what she was saying?

"How many times has he done that?"

"Mo` dan I knows. Cause he were doin` it long fo` I moved hereabouts. But he done did ten or twelve what I knows of since I been heah. Dat's why didn't nobody live in dat house o` your'n and why it's so hard t` rent out. He got bof of de last two cullud girls what lived deah - takin` de same walk you takes."

"Did they live there alone?"

"Lands, no! Dey had men folks, same as you got. Nice young peoples. Naw, dey wasn't alone. But what diffunce dat make to Pattison? He da white man. He do what he want. An` what he want is dem young, sweet, cullud gals.

"We jest thought you was crazy, brave, or desprit. One or de oduh. We didn't even guess you didn't know nothin` 'bout Pattison. Oh, girl, he done got five girls in a fambly way what I knows of."

Ruth-Ann sat still.

This couldn't be true. She felt something disconnect. It

121

seemed as if the room and the air shifted. Her head swam. *I will not let it be true.*

"If everybody knows this, why don't they try to do something about it?"

"Like what? He de white man and dey is cullud girls. What's any somebody gwinter do? If a cullud man touch him, dat's de en ob de cullud man. Dey'll kill him. An ain't no white man gwineter lift a finga 'bout it. Certainly not de sheriff. So ain't nuttin` t` do 'ceptin` t` stay away from him an` keep dat house out yonder empty."

*Our house.*

She finished the lemonade.

What was she going to do?

She wasn't sure she believed Mrs. Wabash. She knew how rural country folk had a way of making up fanciful tales. For all she knew Effy Pattison might be the remnants of a legend told as far back as slavery times. The old man of the woods. She'd heard lots of variations on it. "The boogey man." She didn't know. She knew for sure that in all her walks to and from work she had never seen anyone in the woods.

"Thank you for the lemonade, Mrs. Wabash," said Ruth-Ann. "I don't think I'd have made it all the way home without it." She got to her feet. "And I'll keep an eye out."

"You welcome. An` you do dat, Miz Wenders. An` I'll keep a eye out, too. I don't want dat nasty ol` man gittin` his dirty fingers on you."

Ruth-Ann stepped back into the heat.

She knew one thing. Whether there was an Effy Pattison or not, she wasn't going to say a word about it to Stephen. She remembered the ugly, black thread, the zig-zag stitches so plain

122

holding the halves of Calter's neck together in the coffin.

She knew the Wenders craziness. She lived with Stephen every day.

Usually, she didn't see the craziness. But it was always there, just beneath the surface. It was what could drive him to be away from his new bride five months out of the year. Relentless. It would not abide what other people took for granted. It did not accept what had to be accepted as the very prerequisites for life.

In the unremitting heat, with her country girl's eyes, she watched the undergrowth painstakingly. She was not going to let anything take her by surprise. She knew the responsibility was hers. Her husband could not know of her peril.

# 27

As Ruth-Ann polished the Fleetwright silverware, she tried to put her misgivings in perspective. First of all, she did not know if there really were an Effy Pattison or whether it were some old, slavery tale. Yet Mrs. Wabash said she *knew* of ten or twelve girls the monster attacked. *Knew.* She said she had *seen him* not long ago. *Seen him.* The woman had no reason to lie. *She* believed it. That was definite. Lavinia had seen *something.* Maybe *not* a possum.

It was also true that Ruth-Ann herself had never seen anyone. In the past three days she had been extremely watchful. She had good eyes. She knew how to look. Nothing. Even this morning coming to work. Nothing.

Mrs. Wabash had also said there hadn't been an attack in some time. Perhaps the old man had become feeble. How old was he anyway? He couldn't continue to be strong enough to overpower robust young women indefinitely. Maybe all the lead had run out of his pencil. Maybe that's why Mrs. Wabash had seen him. He was making his swan song. Maybe by now he was dead. There was no point in getting scared until she knew she had reason to be scared - *still* had reason to be scared. She was tired of being scared of white-men. Now some white man she hadn't even seen. Effy Pattison. No. She was not going to let herself be scared until she knew she had something to be scared of.

She'd been frightened enough in her life.

Nightmare.

Hoppy-Toad.

There was time to have an end of it.

I am going to be like a detective, she thought. I am going to be like Sherlock Holmes. I am going to look for every clue. And if I can't find anything, I'm going to know there is nothing to worry about. Then I'll put this whole, crazy thing out of my mind.

*

Across the little, square, wooden table, with the coal-oil lantern close by him, Stephen sat with a piece of paper in front of him. His chin was pointed up and his eyes seemed to be staring into the darkness above him. Every now and then he dropped his chin, looked at the paper, and wrote something on it. Then, gradually, his chin raised up again, and his eyes fixed on the invisible gloom.

Ruth-Ann knew he was making a list of things to pack. It amused her that he could be so methodical, so organized, yet so hopelessly messy. She smiled. She liked the way the lamp lit up his face while the back side of him seemed only shadow, as if it were joined to the unbroken dark behind him.

"Stephen," she said.

He didn't move.

"Stephen Wenders."

He moved his eyelids.

His eyes let loose of the dark.

He looked at her. He smiled.

She smiled back.

"Huh," he asked.

"What's it like up North?"

He closed his eyes.

125

He opened them again to look at her.

"It's different," he said. He knew she didn't want a quick answer. She wanted a story. She often wanted this particular story, so he smiled and started thinking about how to tell it in a new way.

"When I say it's different, he said, "I mean that in two ways. One way is, it's different from here. It's not as hot in the summer - or as humid, either. There aren't nearly so many colored folks - and it's more ... modern. Modern. Yes. There are more automobiles. More streets are paved. More streetcars. It's faster. The life is faster. People even talk faster. They walk faster, too. Everything. There's a different pace of life. It's hard to adjust at first. The people are not as ... solicitous. Somehow they're more distant.

"Colored - who live on the place - as an everyday matter, the only other Colored they see are those who live and work on the same place. If they want to see other Colored people, they have to make special arrangements. Because those places where they are working, are far removed from where most colored live. That's very different from here.

"So, that's one way I mean that the North is different. It's different from here.

"The other thing I mean when I say, 'It's different,' is that places in the North are different from each other. They're not all the same. So - what it's like - depends on where you are. Near the Ocean - Cape Cod or Long Island - it's cooler. Lots of wind. And the smell of the sea. Only different. It's a northern ocean you smell. It's still got the sea-smell in it. It's nice. But it's not the *same* sea-smell. Grand houses. Summer cottages they call them - though they're bigger than the Fleetwright place - but they still call them summer *cottages!*" He laughed. "Lots of space between them. You might not be able to see your neighbor's house.

126

"But, usually, if they have a cottage on the Cape or Long Island, their main house will be in Boston or New York. I'm not talking about the place they have in the South. That's for winters. Their main house of houses - will be in Boston or New York. You talk about cities - Jacksonville doesn't come close. Jacksonville doesn't know what a city is. Boston is a city. New York is a city. Chicago is a city. If the family's home is in, say, New York, they will stay there until maybe the end of June, then the wife and children go to the cottage until the end of August. The husband comes up on the weekends.

"If they live, say, in Chicago, the summer cottage might be on the Upper Peninsula of Michigan, Northern Wisconsin, or Sault St. Marie. The Great Lakes. There's no ocean. It's wilder than the Cape or Long Island. Full of black flies and hungry mosquitoes. Not as many people, either. But beautiful. No ocean, but lakes and rivers and forests.

"For us, the work up there is not too different from what it is here, but - as I said - the pace is different.

"Colored tend to live in pockets in the biggest cities. They have their own life, apart from whites. Not like here. Northern Negroes are ... well, less subservient." He laughed. "More like my Daddy. They think they have the same rights as anybody else.

"And, then, of course," he knew what she wanted to hear. As usual he had saved it. Still, he said it differently every time, so - though it was what she wanted to hear - it would sound new.

"There's no jim-crow. Not enough colored for there to be any point in it. Shop where you want. Ride where you want. There are a few 'whites only' signs and 'colored' signs, but not *everywhere*. Of course, the newspaper advertisements for work or a place to rent let you know right off, 'no colored need apply,' or 'whites only.' And northern white people don't love Negroes, but ... I guess one of the main things is ... you don't have to be afraid all the time. Any white person - boy or girl, man or woman, old or infirm, crazy or stupid - does not pose the same perpetual, whimsical threat over you - over your life. That if you look at them wrong, or say the wrong thing, or they just don't happen to feel good, your life is not at stake.

"None of the families I work for even make you use the back door. And, it's like - when you're shopping or boarding a train, people will sometimes call you Mr. or Mrs. So sometimes you feel different about yourself as a human being. As if ... as if being a Negro didn't make you any the less. I want you to feel that, Ruth-Ann. I want you to know it."

He did not know how that was going to happen if he went North every summer while she stayed home. He did not know how she could get to know it.

He was quiet for a minute. They both were.

"Ruth-Ann?"

She looked at him.

He didn't know how to say it without letting her know he was afraid, but he had to say it.

"When I'm gone ... you think Lavinia would come here to stay with you?"

Ruth-Ann blinked.

It was a brilliant idea. And it was all his own. She hadn't had to say a thing, not even hint.

Her face lit up.

She rushed around the table and hugged him. "Oh, Stephen, that's a wonderful idea!"

# 28

One thing Ruth-Ann had never done, despite all her surveillance, was walk into the woods. She had acted as if the forest were an actual wall, as if the fastness of the wooded interior could not be breached. The absence of any clear entryway fostered that illusion. It would not be possible simply to follow a path into the bush. There weren't any. She would have to force her way through thick undergrowth and climb downed logs with prickly branches and twigs. That could not be done with stealth. Anyone hiding could hear her coming a long way off. She could not catch anybody by surprise.

She laughed at herself. *What would she do if she did catch somebody by surprise?*

Run she hoped. Run and scream.

But not to Stephen.

No.

Lavinia?

When she came. If she came. What would Lavinia do? At least there would be two of them. Why not wait till Lavinia came to peek into those woods? What if she couldn't come? In any case, what was to be gained from such dirty, sweaty, prickly work as poking around in the woods?

She did not know. She would not know until she tried.

She made up her mind that on Saturday afternoon, on her way home from work, she would make her first sally into the woods.

Not far.  Not far.  But to get the feel for it, to see if it "felt like" someone was prowling around in there.

She reached her conclusion on Friday morning, soon after she arrived at the Fleetwright's.  Her courage was high.  By early Saturday afternoon when the execution of her decision was only a few hours away, she was terrified.

\*

She wasn't aware of it, but Ruth-Ann's pace was somewhat more restrained than usual as she came down her road Saturday afternoon.  In fact, the longer she walked, the more slowly she moved.  She hadn't decided exactly where she would try to penetrate the green wall.  There were no breaks, but there were some places that looked less dense than others.  She wanted to be sure she was past the line-of-sight from the Wabash house before she made her attempt.  She wanted no witness to this venture - at least none she knew of.

A quarter mile past the Wabash's house she began to look closely into the undergrowth.

Where?

Where?

She saw, at last, what seemed to be a faint depression.  She walked over to it, through the tall weeds lining the road, stopped, and examined the place.  Yes, it was a natural channel that carried water from the road when there was a heavy rain.  If she took off her shoes, left them by the roadside, lifted up her skirt, and got down on her knees, she could squeeze under a huge log that spanned the depression.  The ground was squishy, but her bare feet wouldn't mind.

She looked up and down the road.

She scanned the forest.

She stood absolutely still.

No one.

She took off her shoes and placed them neatly just off the road. They wouldn't catch any body's attention. She dropped to her knees and disappeared into the tall grass. Seconds later she stretched herself under the log. When she got to its far side, she stood up. She heard, immediately, the mosquitoes swarming for her. She looked down for a clear place to step, where she could clamber up out of the ditch.

That is when she saw on the channel bottom, in the one clear oval of mud, the footprint.

Well-defined.

Fresh, not a full day old. A man's huge, naked foot.

She forgot all about mosquitoes. She was under the log and out of the woods in a wink. She grabbed her shoes and ran a good quarter of a mile before she started walking again. Her pace was no longer restrained. After awhile she stopped to put her shoes back on.

Now she knew. Somebody was in there. Maybe it wasn't Pattison. But somebody frequented those woods. She had evidence now. The question was, what was she going to do with it?

# 29

Time was on Ruth-Ann's side. She did not have to keep her knowledge from Stephen for long because he would be gone. But the knowledge was so big inside her she did not know how she was going to keep it down even the short time she had left. She had not seen the man, but her eyes were getting more practiced. She had seen more signs of him. The Sherlock Holmes in her was strengthening. The evidence was becoming ever more irresistible. When Lavinia came, at least she could tell her. But they had not heard from her.

Ruth-Ann made it part of her regular routine to stop by Mrs. Wabash's house on the way home. They shared notes on Effy. It was a way to relieve the tension. Luckily, she slept less. When she did sleep, she collapsed. No Nightmare. No Hoppy-Toad.

One evening as she waited by the window facing the road, as she waited, eyes on the roadway's rutty surface and the shadowed wood, waited in terror for Stephen to come home, to be with her, to put his arms around her, she confirmed to herself that she had to continue to bear her burden in secret. She knew she could hold on a little longer. Until her husband was delivered from this hellish place. Until then she could hang on. Until then she *would* hang on.

*Oh, Stephen just come home soon and hold me again in your*

*arms so we can be together another time and I can banish all these*
*dreadful fears from my heart.*

Stephen didn't know why they hadn't heard from Lavinia. Sometimes it took the mail a while to get out to these country places. Maybe that was it. What they were both afraid of, but did not mention, was the flu. Lord, don't let that girl have it. Stephen's time to leave was near. If they didn't hear from her in a couple of days he was going to have to drive out there to find out.

*

The time was coming. Effraim could tell. He'd teased himself with her long enough. He'd savored the anticipation of her long enough. Now the very sight of her drove him into fits of delirium. He had to have her.

He laughed long and wildly. He knew all her patterns, all of her comings and goings. He knew when and where it would be quickest and safest to grab her.

She could not escape.

# 30

The gloom cast by the brooding trees on the left side of the road seemed to swallow Ruth-Ann.

Stephen would be gone in three days. Tomorrow he was going to see about Lavinia.

What if she couldn't come? Ruth-Ann was terrified. She didn't know what she would do.

Her feet dragged through the dust. The way home had never seemed so long. Hot. *And it's not even summer yet. What's it going to be like when summer gets here? When I am alone, without Stephen, walking down this miserable road that seems to have no end, a lunatic white man hiding behind the trees watching me. I will be too hot to care. Too wretched to care.* She was sweating heavily. The dampness surrounding her and sticking to her made her imagine she was wearing a shroud.

She wanted to run up and down the road screaming. The sun broiled her. She threw her head back. Her mouth fell open. She brought her head forward. Lights, spots, seemed to dance before her eyes. She found it hard to breathe. She took deep breaths. She felt cold in the heat as sweat poured from her in streams. Bright on one side, dark on the other. Her eyes could make no finer discernments. Light and dark, with the bright spots dancing between them, moving from shadow to radiance and back again.

*

Effraim Patterson waited for the girl to draw nearer. Even from this distance he could tell there was something different about the way she moved. Her dress was sticking to her. It revealed her whole body. Breasts. Stomach. Hips. Thighs. He giggled.
His.
Spittle collected in the corners of his mouth.
His.
Dark stains streaked the dress under her arms where sweat was running like a river.
*He would dip into it, dip into that river.*
He licked his lips.
His erection was so strong it made him shudder.
The throbbing in his chest was almost painful.
He breathed heavily.
She came one slow step at a time.
There was no music to her movement as there had always been before. It was almost as if her feet could not free themselves from the road's surface and had to pull themselves along it. Weaving, weaving all over the road. She was slumped.
Without being able to see the expression on her face, Effraim knew by her posture, by her rate of progress, by her gate, by her lagging perambulation, that she was down, down as he had never seen her. He had seen her hot before, tired. He had seen her worn-

out. He had seen her so often in such varied moods he'd believed he'd seen her full range of dispositions. No. Today was different. He moved infinitesimally forward.

As his eyes locked on her, registering every bit of datum she emitted, as his senses honed in on her, as his nervous system attuned itself to her and fired off its neurons, as calculations and messages and sensations clicked in his brain, an involuntary grin - like a death rictus - spread his smile from cheekbone to cheekbone.

He knew.

The information told him.

Conclusively.

*She was vulnerable.*

He became transformed. From a watcher to a doer. Almost at once. Silently. Stealthily. With practiced mastery. Invisible in the wooded undergrowth. He began to move.

*

Blind and deaf, Ruth-Ann staggered forward. Her lungs cried out for air but air would not enter them.

***Sound!***

Broke into her consciousness. But it did not come through her ears. It came through her chest. Staccato. Then silence. Staccato. Then nothing.

Thump-thump.

O No!

Her eyes opened.

She could see.

On the road ahead of her - *not behind her* - ahead of her.

Coming towards her.

An instant of sound. Then nothing. Coming. Thump-thump. Eyes riveted on her.

Closer. Large. Frothing at the mouth. She could smell it. White and squirmy. Holding onto something long and shiny and red between its legs, pointed at her.

A guttural noise came out of it as it lurched upon her.

She screamed.

"Hoppy-Toad! Hoppy-Toad!"

Like wings her voice gave her motion. She fled across the road and down the spit of sand.

"Hoppy-Toad! Hoppy-Toad!"

She did not see the white jets shooting after her as the white slimy thing squeezed the long, red, shiny protuberance and fell down in the road, writhing in the dust.

*

Raging, howling, laughing, shrieking, Effraim crashed through the woods towards his house. His careful, practiced, planned pattern of indiscernible passage abandoned, he kicked rocks aside, trampled vines, broke branches, plowed through thickets. He wasn't concerned. He knew that in a few days the forest's regrowth would cover the turnpike he was gouging out of it.

He was ecstatic.

*Oh, yes, oh, yes. She's seen it now. She knows what she's got comin' to her. It's going to be on her mind.* A wild gale of laughter swept out of him.

*Oh, I've taken her to the limit! I've taken her to the limit! This will be my crowning glory!*

He re-pictured the voluptuous sight of her before him,

137

staggering, helpless, all her female parts exposed by the dress held to them by perspiration.

*I almost got carried away. Almost took it too far. I did. Such a heat overcame me, such a boiling in my loins, I would have taken her right there in the dust on the road. I lost control. If she'd kept standing there, I would have taken her - right there. Too soon. Lucky, she ran. Just when I was about to jump on her, she ran.*

He bellowed berserkly. He shouted out loud. "That makes it perfect! That makes it perfect!"

*The next time we meet face-to-face, I will be the incarnation of her worst nightmare.*

Howling with glee he approached his house.

He went to the back where he'd tied up the chicken in the morning.

He wasted no motions. He grabbed its feet, untied it, with one stroke of the axe, chopped off its head. He raised the bird with its neck spurting blood above his head and let the hot, bright fluid, gush down over him into his hair and onto his face into his beard, over his shoulders and down his body.

Then he plunged his spewing manhood into the blood-pumping hole. He fell on top of the headless chicken, grabbing it, mashing it with his hands, rolling over and over it in the dirt. He stood up screaming,

"Now, she'll be mine! Now, she'll be mine!"

He tore off into the woods, running into trees, getting knocked onto his back, raising up, racing until he was knocked down again.

Finally he stood over a creek-bed and bayed like a coon-hound.

*She's got a husband,* he thought, *but she's not his anymore.*

138

# 31

Locked inside, Ruth-Ann looked out of the window facing the road. She saw only the dark forest. No animal. No person. Nothing moved. Silent. Except for the sound of the water in the bay behind her. And the beating of her heart. She stared. She would have to venture out on the road tomorrow on the way to work. And all the days after that with Stephen gone.

Tomorrow - oh, my God - he would be gone to see Lavinia.

She clenched her fists in the curtains.

She could not.

She could not.

*He waited for her. Old and stringy and foul. White, and red, and squirming. Waiting.*

*There was nothing she could do to stop him. Nothing.*

By herself in the house she screamed and screamed and screamed.

When Stephen came home she still stood in the window. Her face was stark. She held the curtains in a death-grip.

He had to pry her loose to hold her.

"What's wrong, my darling."

*I can't tell him. He's crazy and he'll do something crazy and he'll get himself killed.*

*I can't tell him.*

139

She clung to him.

Her nails, short and stubby though they were, dug through his shirt and broke the skin on his arms. He held her more tightly.

"What's wrong?"

She pushed her head into his chest, pushed until she could feel the bone of his chest, hard, against the bone of her head.

"Please ... tell me."

*No.*

*No.*

*That's the last thing I can do.*

"Just hold me, Stephen. Please. Hold me."

He held her.

He was conscious of her face pressed into his chest and the tears from her face dampening his pectoral muscles and running down his stomach. He felt the contours of her back and the small of her back under his hands. He heard her sniffle and he felt the warmth of her breath. Her legs were flush against his. He turned and lowered his cheek to the soft, crinkly texture on top of her head.

"Is it because I'm going away?"

Her body shook with sobbs.

He held her even more tightly.

"It's alright, Ruth-Ann. It's alright. I'll be back. We're man and wife now."

She knew as she clung to him even more desperately that there was only one way he'd be back. If she told him nothing. Which meant she knew her fate. She had to face it.

She shook uncontrollably.

He guided her to the bed where they sat down. She was welded to him, sobbing and slobbering.

He had never seen her like this.

140

He brought his right hand up from her back and stroked the top of her head. He bent down and kissed her forehead. He held her again with both hands, resting his chin on her forehead.

"I know it hurts, honey. It hurts me, too. But it's not going to be that bad."

She saw the old white man dancing on the road, his eyes alight, burning. She saw him reach out his hands for her, his fingers clutched like talons. She saw his dirty, matted hair, his filthy whiskers clotted with abominations. His open mouth held gapped, crooked, broken, pitted, yellowed teeth. Spittle oozed from the corners of his lips down into his beard. He came so close to her the sharpness of his vile smell had forced her to stop breathing. Flies hovered around him, lighted on him. Then he had reached into his pants and pulled out that horrid, jutting thing.

"Oh, no!"

She pulled back her face from Stephen's chest.

"Oh, no," she screamed again.

"I can't! I can't. I can't do it!"

He took her face into his hands.

He looked down into her tormented features.

"Can't do what, darling?"

Through her sobs she told him three times before he began to understand.

The first time she told him, he could not even make out what she was saying, her voice so full of tears, going low, almost inaudible, and then almost shrieking. Then, no words at all. Until the words came out again, more like sobs than words, weeping, bleeding words. Wounded words. He held her, patted her. Coaxed her.

"Please. My little flower. Slowly. Take your time. Tell me

141

again."

She did. More coherent.

This time, he didn't want to understand. He couldn't make himself believe it. *He must be hearing wrong. That he had brought her, brought his wife, to this place of horrors. Oh, no. It could not be. He must have misheard her. She could not be saying what he thought she had said.* He felt ice running through him. It was not heat. It was cold rage. "Please ..." he asked one more time.

She told him the third time, crying all the way through it, but this time, plain, very plain.

His mind hardened.

His body hardened.

He wanted to push her away.

To walk to the kitchen, grab the butcher knife, run across the road, into the forest, find the white man, and cut him down, cut him down, cut him down!

He wanted to push her away.

This was no time for thinking and talking.

This was a time for acting.

He wanted to push her away.

But he could not. He had to keep holding her. She needed him.

The craziness was coming on.

She felt it and couldn't let it.

Her fingers relaxed her hold on him. She caressed him.

"I need you here with me, Stephen. I'm afraid to be alone. Don't leave me. Don't step out of that door. I need you here, in this house. With me."

He squeezed her.

"I know."

142

She held him tightly again, this time not digging in her nails. "Stephen, he'll get me. You have t`go to work tomorrow, and talk t` Lavinia. Even if you don't go to work or to see Lavinia. Even if you go looking for him, you can't find him in one day. He knows those woods. He'll hide. You'll be in the woods looking for him. I'll be on the road coming home - and he'll grab me. If he doesn't get me tomorrow, the next day you'll be gone with the Northrups. He'll be free to get me. Any time he wants - any time he wants, Stephen. I can't stay heah. I've got t` go. Tomorrow. I cain't go home, Daddy would act just as crazy as the Harrises - or you!"

Stephen realized she was right. *He could do nothing. As nothing had been done before. That's why the man was still there. Nothing could be done about him. Still there. There was only one thing he could do. What she said. Get her out. He hated that. He didn't want to run from this man just because he was white.*

Ruth-Ann ran her small hands up and down over his shoulder blades. She kissed his chest through his shirt.

"Stephen, Stephen," she said. "We can't do anything about that white man."

At last it was Stephen in his impotence who cried.

He knew what he had to do. It came to him, as in a vision. It was, now, the only way to fight this pale spawn of Satan himself.

\*

They left early in the morning. Stephen drove all the way across the county from Essie Pattison's woods, into the remote area the old man knew nothing about, to the farm carved out of the deep

143

wilderness where the wild Wenders lived. He took her home to his people, where, although he would be far away, the responsibility for her would be him and his. There she would wait, nurtured in the bosom of those beautiful, crazy people, while, unknown to Stephen, their first child quickened in her womb.

*The Wenders*
*Wintertime 1917*

# 32

Persephone, Jenina, Agatha, and Euridyce rolled on the ground. Tears ran down their faces and their ribs ached. One by one, they sat up. Ruth-Ann sat, Indian-style, surrounded by them, a bewildered expression on her face.

Jenina put her hand on Ruth-Ann's shoulder. "I have never seen a look on anybody's face like what was on yours when you and Stephen stepped out of those woods."

The sisters started laughing again. The look on Ruth-Ann's face remained just as perplexed.

Agatha laid on her back and hooted.

As the noise subsided, Ruth-Ann said, in defense of herself, "Well, I just, I ... didn't know where I was."

That got them started again.

At last, Jenina said, "Well, girl, you're at the Wenders'.

\*

It seemed to Ruth-Ann as if she and Stephen had walked half a day through deep woods, occasional low-lying branches batting their faces, continually beset by every buzzing, biting, and sucking insect known to human kind. The cart-track was rough, which made walking hard on both the ankles and the feet. Their clothes were soaked with perspiration.

The trees and undergrowth were so dense that only a few

yards of the track were ever visible. It wound and twisted, never seeming to go straight for more than a few steps. Ruth-Ann couldn't tell if they had been going in circles.

All at once a cacophony of sound burst upon them. Ruth-Ann stopped. Stephen went on for maybe thirty more feet before he realized she wasn't beside him. He turned around.

She stood stock-still. Never had she heard such a bedlam of noise. When she concentrated on the sounds, she could make out geese honking; ducks quacking; dogs howling, barking, and baying; mules braying; cows lowing. But mostly what she heard was awful, terrible, discordant volume. She could not see the source of the blizzard of sound. Shattered, almost hysterical with thirst, fatigue, twisted ankles, sore feet, sweat, bug bites, and frustration, she refused to take another step.

Stephen strode back to her. He kissed her forehead.

"We're almost there," he said. "That's our welcoming committee."

They broke free from the woods into a vast clearing. Dogs raced madly about, loosing every manner of canine holler. A troop of geese marched resolutely towards them. Various other creatures, out of sight, lent their voices to the pandemonium.

In stark contrast, elegantly dressed women and men stood in a straight line, at attention, in front of the most convoluted, twisted, ramshackle, and comical house Ruth-Ann had ever seen. Once again she stopped.

It was then that the line of people began to walk towards her, across the open ground, shooing creatures.

The house was as crazy as it first appeared. It did not take Ruth-Ann long to learn its history - at least various parts of it - as everyone was eager to share a favorite story. Somewhere in the midst of the jumble was the original house Mr. Wenders had built for his bride, Ona. Where, exactly, was no longer possible to discern. Papa, as everyone in the family called Mr. Wenders, had added onto the house whenever he saw the need, wherever and however it pleased him, and with whatever materials were at hand. Frequently, the additions were a room at a time - for another child, a storage space, a closet. Some additions had doors of their own to the outside. Some were inaccessible from inside the house. All the add-ons were of various shapes and sizes, joined at all kinds of angles, some even standing on top of others.

Stephen and Ruth-Ann were designated a room, with the understanding that Ruth-Ann would be its sole occupant while Stephen was away to the North. It was one of the rooms with its own door to the outside, though it also connected with the main body of the house through another door.

Despite Mr. Wenders' fierce appearance, it did not take Ruth-Ann long to learn who ruled the household. Mama Ona, as Mrs. Wenders was known, not only by her family, but by anyone who had any reason to be acquainted with the Wenders, was indisputably in-charge. She was a physically imposing woman with strong opinions and a will of iron. She would not be challenged, and she was not. The number one rule in the Wenders homestead was that no one was accepted into the household without Mama Ona's personal approval. Her standard for family membership was so high that no one had ever met it. That's why all her grown children - with the now notable exception of Stephen - had never married.

The girls were all ravishing beauties and the boys handsome as princes. Every one - women and men - had their picks of the most promising members of the opposite sex. No one was good enough. Their mother's preferences did not prevent the younger Wenders from falling in love with lesser mortals. They did - sometimes deeply. But, respectively, after each such candidate was presented to Mama Ona, the children learned that the prospective spouse had failed to make the grade. This verdict often did not result in the termination of the romance, but it meant that everyone knew that the whole matter was a dead-end.

Because of Mama Ona's supreme authority, this continual death knell of lost loves did not result in any tension within the Wenders household, but it did result in tremendous tensions within each child. With Stephen as the oldest, his frequent absences required by the movement of his employers from South to North, gave him a kind of *de facto* independence. It was not a condition anyone would ever comment on, but it was real. It was strengthened by Mama Ona's great reluctance to deny her first child his heart's desire.

# 33

While Stephen attended high school, and worked in Jacksonville to support himself, at one store where he worked, when everyone had left for the day, he practiced on the typewriter. It was one of the proudest possessions of the store's owner, Herman Feemdstead. Mr. Feemstead, however, could not operate it. He purchased it out of sheer vanity. It sat in his office, as a shining ornament of his success. Every evening, when no one was around, Stephen sat down at the wondrous instrument and sent it through its paces at lightning speed.

One night, Jasper Hanks, a notable town vagrant, wandering up and down alleyways familiar to him, besotted by cheap spirits, heard an infernal clattering and clicking racket. At first, he could not tell where the noise was coming from, as it seemed to be coming from everywhere. Fortified by alcohol, he focused his remaining consciousness on locating the source of the intolerable sound. He eventually excluded every possibility except the back of Feemstead's store. He stumbled up to the back door. The door itself was open, but as Jasper found out by pushing and pulling, the screen was hooked - no doubt to prevent visitors like Jasper from coming in out of the alley. The place was clearly the source of the noise. Jasper could hardly manage to stand at the door in the face of that intolerable clacking. But stand he did. The screen, aided by the formidable hooch, made it very difficult for Jasper to see anything at all in the room, or to make sense of what he saw. But after a long time he discerned that the noise came from ... a nigger ... something Feemstead's nigger was doing. He was sitting at a table, making

149

motions, and producing sounds worse than howling, fighting, alley cats.

Jasper bent over and decided he was just going to keep looking until he figured out what the nigger was up to. His vision did not improve, but after awhile it came to him what was on the table where the nigger was doing his fooling. It was the gadget Feemstead was so proud of that he showed it off to everybody. Jasper couldn't remember exactly what it was called. But he remembered what Feemstead said about it. It could write. It was some kind of writing machine. Feemstead also said it was high-fangled, new. Didn't nobody know how to use it. But here was that ... nigger ... making it jump and pop, looking right at home with it. Jasper's ears started burning. *There's some things white men cain't tolerate*, he thought, as he lurched away from the door and staggered down the alley. *There's some things what defies the laws of man and God, and what we's got t` put a stop to. The nigger have gone too far.* He set out to find some white men to set things right.

That's how the mob came to kick in the screen door, snatch Stephen out from behind the table, pummel him, tie him up, and drag him along the ground to a big live oak a block off the city square.

By the time the crowd reached the tree, it had drawn all kinds of white people, excited by the spectacle, by the ritual re-enactment of their heritage. They put the noose around Stephen's neck and stood him up on a table while one man climbed the tree to fasten the rope securely onto the overhanging limb. The people shouted wildly to each other?

"What'd the nigga do?"

"I don't know."

"I don't know, neither, but whatever it were, he ain't gon` do it no more!"

150

Much whooping and hollering.

"From what I heard tell he got messed up in white folks' business."

"Doin` what?"

"I don't exacklee know."

"I heard tell he was usin` a writin` machine."

"A what?"

"A writin` machine."

"I ain't nevuh heard of sech."

"A writin` machine!"

"Kill the nigga!"

"I'm a white man and I ain't never heard tell of no writin` machine."

"Kill the nigga!"

"What you think we `bout t` do, Harry?"

People laughed. Some were near delerium.

A large man at the edge of the crowd overheard some of the conversation. He began pushing his way through the people. He tried to get a good look at the Black man standing on the table. He got closer. He asked the man beside him, "Ain't that Feemstead's nigger?"

"How would I know?"

The man kept pushing and asking.

Finally someone answered, "Yeah, he the one. He the uppity darky `bout t` git hisself killed."

"Hey! Hey!" The big man started shouting and shoving people aside more aggressively.

People turned around to see who was making such a ruckus.

Some moved to get away from his rough hands. He pushed and shoved right to the edge of the crowd.

151

"Hey - Wentworth, Brady," he shouted.

"Who's that - oh, it's you, Jason Wenders."

"Yeah, it's me. Y'all cain't kill that boy!"

People started laughing.

"You just watch us."

"Naw, now, I cain't let you do it. He's my cousin. His daddy is my father's half-brother. I cain't let you do it.

"Y'all caught any other nigger usin` a typewriter, I'd say, go ahead, string him up. But I cain't let you kill my father's nephew while I just stand here and watch. He's a Wenders!"

\*

Jason Wenders was the only thing that kept Stephen from dying that night. So Mama Ona had a soft spot for her eldest. When he announced he was going to marry this little, ol` gal he had met in Jacksonville, everybody's eyes or ears had turned to Mama Ona. They waited for her to explode. But she didn't say anything. She didn't say yes or no. She didn't utter a word on it. Everybody was stunned.

A few weeks later, she gave Stephen her blessing. She still hadn't seen the girl, but she gave him her blessing. Nobody knew what to make of it. Indeed, she didn't meet Ruth-Ann until the wedding. Everybody else fell in love with the new bride right away, but it was hard to know what went on in Mama Ona's head.

152

Besides Stephen, only one other child was missing from the Wenders farmstead, Naomi. As Lavinia had aptly said, all the Wenders children were frighteningly beautiful, but even amidst such stunning good-looks, Naomi stood out. She had conquered Jacksonville. Men literally fell down on their knees before her. With such a reception, she no longer felt a need to reside at the backwoods farm house, far from society. She visited rarely.

Something about those two elder children kept them from Mama Ona's control. She more than made up for it with the others. There was a big question about how she was going to treat Ruth-Ann, not her birth-child, but a daughter-*in-law* - young, still a girl, destined to bear Mama Ona's first grandchild, and resident beneath her roof. The Wenders siblings were all eager to see.

Ruth-Ann wrote Lavinia and Essie to tell them she had moved, and to explain why. She also shared the news about her pregnancy. Their replies were ecstatic, concealing the twinge of jealousy each felt.

# 34

The Wenders' new family member saw Papa Wenders probably less than she saw anyone else. The farm was large and there was always something for him to do, often on its peripheries. He had Sunday dinner with the family, but aside from that, he only got home for dinner or supper two or three times a week. Sometimes he was working around the house and couldn't afford the time to stop. Other times he was out of earshot or eyesight, looking after the cows, cutting down trees, pulling stumps, hunting varmits, or coming back from a long trek to town. Ruth-Ann took a liking to him. Unlike most of his children, he didn't talk much. But he didn't need to. Simply his presence was reassuring. It felt good to know he was around.

Ruth-Ann soon relieved him of one of his most irksome tasks. The Wenders installed her as their chief snake-killer. Whenever they spotted one they'd holler, "Ruth-Ann! Come kill this snake!" They all knew how, but - like Papa - Ruth-Ann was very good at it, so they stopped traipsing through the woods to find Papa when they saw a snake near the house. They just called Ruth-Ann.

The first outsiders Ruth-Ann saw enter the clearing surprised her. The house was so far in the deep woods she expected she'd never see anybody on the farm except family. But she learned that every now and then, groups of four or five would come trucking through the trees and swamps. Mama Ona knew roots. She knew herbs and potions. Some said, though never to Mama Ona's face, that she was a conjur-woman. Everybody *knew* she was a mid-wife, and occasionally one of her sons would drive the wagon down the mule-track with her sitting beside him, her bag behind her in the wagon-well. Sometimes she'd be gone all day, sometimes longer. People came a little more than usual because of the killer flu. They wanted protection, even a *chance* for protection. Many believed that Mama Ona off in the woods was the root doctor who could keep the evil away. If Mama Ona was away doing midwifery, they waited. They'd wait for days if they had to. She was their hope in a dangerous world.

Agatha and Euridyce were in awe of Ruth-Ann. They were closest to her in age and were the most natural to befriend her. But they seemed so much younger, both to themselves and everybody else. Ruth-Ann had lived in the world. She was married to their oldest brother. She was about to have a baby. In every way, she was a woman. Comparatively they were children. They liked to be around her. They sat next to her at the table, and joined her in the chores. Sometimes they showed her around the farm or walked with her in the woods. Often they just sat next to her when she was cooking, sewing, or reading a book. In fact, she got them reading and often the three of them settled under a tree, each with her own book.

The Wenders boys - all grown men - were home for every meal, but the rest of the time they were away from the house - off with their father doing some farm work, or chores of their own, keeping the cart-track free, tending the cattle, horses, and mules, chopping and hauling wood, fishing, and hunting. Occasionally, one of them would hire himself out to earn some cash money for the family. Tims and Solders seemed particularly suited to life in the deep woods. But Ernest was patterning himself after his oldest brother. He wanted to leave the farm and go into the city, to live the big life ... as soon as he could get up the nerve. He had shared his ambition only with Stephen who had told him he would get him on with a family in Jacksonville as soon as he was ready. Of course, that would have to be some time when Stephen was actually in Jacksonville and not somewhere up North. How Ernest wanted to go up *there*, to see what it was like.

Justis did his share of the chores. He did them hard and fast, all at one time, to get them over with. He spent most of his time in his room or out in a special shed he'd built, working on one of his contraptions. "Inventions," he called them. His room and the shed were full of them. Others were scattered about the clearing surrounding the farm house. Nobody ever asked him what they were, because he was only too happy to describe every detail and feature in the minutest detail, as well as what they did, why they made so much sense, and how much money he was going to make off of them. He liked Ruth-Ann right away because she asked him about each device she saw and sat down and listened to him while he explained all its marvels with the most exacting precision.

Everyday Ruth-Ann wrote Stephen. Whenever one of the boys drove the mule-wagon down the cart-track and eventually to Mandarin, to the post office, he'd take the stack of letters she'd written. He'd always come back with a pack of letters for her from Stephen. Ruth-Ann took the letters into her room, *their* room, as she thought of it, and organized them chronologically. She always started with the first letter and read her way to the last. No one bothered her during those times. Anyone who spotted a snake went on and killed it. No shouts for Ruth-Ann.

156

# 35

As Ruth-Ann's belly grew bigger, the whole Wenders household became increasingly excited.

Because Ruth-Ann was the first child in her family, she remembered some of her mother's pregnancies, and in the case of the youngest children, she had helped with them when they were infants. She'd helped with farm animals, too, so births and babies were nothing new to her. Still she was more excited than everybody around her because this was going to be *her* baby. She was also comforted that Mama Ona was a midwife. Many women died in childbirth. Most did not, but some did. It was always a danger. Babies died, too. People didn't like to talk about those things, but everyone knew. Ruth-Ann's mother had lost two babies. The family always tended the little graves, and Ruth-Ann never forgot the two tiny bodies. A boy and a girl.

Because none of Mama Ona's children had given birth, Stephen's baby would be her first grandchild. If anything could be done to save that life, she was going to do it. She didn't intend to put up with the same foolishness that resulted in Stephen's marrying without her permission, without even asking her permission. No more of that. This baby was going to be hers, not the child's who was going to bear it. The girl was barely able to take care of her own self. No, Mama Ona was determined to take over the baby - and the mother, too.

She started advising Ruth-Ann on what to eat and drink, how

to carry herself, what she could do.  She fixed little potions for the mother-to-be.  Some of them were nasty.

"You drink that down, girl.  It's good for you.  Good for the baby, too.  Keep it from bein` born with a cowl."

Mama Ona started studying Ruth-Ann to see whether the baby was going to be a boy or a girl.  Ruth-Ann did not want to know.  She knew Mama Ona had all kinds of ways of discovering such things - how Ruth-Ann carried the baby inside her, the color of the whites of her eyes, the foods she liked to eat.  Mama Ona could learn things from the way Ruth-Ann walked, from the scents of her breath, the texture of her hair, and from the way the baby moved in the womb.  When she midwifed, she could always tell whether the baby was going to be a girl or a boy.  But Ruth-Ann didn't want to know.

Mama Ona kept studying her.  "Stephen's gwinter  see the baby when it's borned," she told Ruth-Ann one morning.  "Baby's gwineter be born late January.  Stephen's gwinter be here in Florida.  Won't be up in  Yankeeland.  He'll see his baby new-borned."  She patted her daughter-in-law on the arm and smiled.

That afternoon as Ruth-Ann and Jenina sat on the porch steps shelling peas, Ruth-Ann said, "I don't want to know if it's going to be a boy or a girl.  I know Mama Ona can tell me, but I don't want to know."

Jenina looked up, surprised.  "Why not?"

She was proud of her mother's ability to tell what a baby was going to be.  She had never missed even once.  In fact, Jenina was eager to know what Ruth-Ann was going to have.

Ruth-Ann stopped snapping and rested her hands in her lap.  "I don't know.  I guess I'm just old-fashioned."

Jenina laughed.  "You mighty young t` be old fashioned."

Both girls started snapping peas again.

"Aren't you curious," asked Jenina.

"Yes." Ruth-Ann paused. "I'm curious. But one thing about it - I'm going to find out. When the baby's born, I'm going to find out. It's not going to stay a secret. And I can wait. I want to wait."

"Hmm. I think Mama wants t` write Stephen and tell him what his baby's going to be."

Ruth-Ann's voice raised involuntarily. "But I'm the baby's mother - it should come from me!"

Jenina laughed. She sneaked a sideways glance at Ruth-Ann. "Now, we see what it is - you're jealous."

A hint of a smile passed over Ruth-Ann's lips. "Maybe. It's my baby and my husband. It ought to come from me."

Jenina nodded. She could understand jealousy.

For awhile there was just the sound of shells snapping.

"Tell her you don't want to know," said Jenina.

"What?"

"I said, tell her you don't want to know."

"Mama Ona? Me - tell Mama Ona?"

"That's right. Tell her you don't want to know."

They continued working.

"But." Ruth-Ann stopped. "That means you couldn't know either. Nobody could know but Mama Ona."

"Why?"

Ruth-Ann laughed. She started working again. "You know you couldn't keep it from me. You'd slip ... one way or another. You wouldn't mean to, but you'd let it slip. So would everybody else. Except Mama Ona. If she doesn't want something to slip, it won't."

"No. It won't," said Jenina. She thought about herself. She

thought about her brothers and sisters, about her father. Ruth-Ann was right. One way or another, it would get out. "But it's your baby. If you don't want to know, tell her. We won't be any worse off than you will. It'll be a surprise for us, too. And as you said, it won't be a secret forever."

They both laughed.

"I don't know," said Ruth-Ann, her fingers working quickly and rhythmically. "How can I say that to Mama Ona?"

"You can say it for the very same reason you told me - it's your baby and it's your husband, and it ought to come from you." Amused, Jenina looked at her young sister-in-law. "You're going to be the mama, not Mama Ona."

They had a syncopation going on between them in the work. Jenina put the second bowl of peas aside and put another between them.

"Jenina ...."

"Uh-huh."

"You never said that to Mama Ona."

"What?"

"That you would like to be the bride - and not her ... that you would be the one who would say yes to Henry, yes to who you would marry ... and not her."

"I know. I know."

"Then why ?"

"Oh, girl. I can't. I just can't. She's Mama-Ona. And that's why I know that you have to. Because if you don't, she'll run your life. Just as she does the rest of us. I can't, Ruth-Ann. I just can't. But you have to."

The peas made no sound as they dropped on top of each other in the bowl.

## 36

Alone, Ruth-Ann walked through the forest. The trail was narrow. She didn't like the whines and clicks of the bugs. She didn't like the mosquitoes or deer flies that found her so sumptuous a meal. She had to keep an eye out for snakes. But she had to be alone. Because she'd thought about it. She'd looked at the Wenders children and she'd thought about them, too. Jenina was right. Ruth-Ann loved Mama Ona, but Jenina was right. Ruth-Ann had to summon up the courage.

It was not cool in the forest, but it was shadowy. The light was dim, the trees kept out unfiltered sun. But it was not cool - too humid, too still, to be cool.

In the midst of whirring and buzzing insects, raucous bird cries and varied whistles, Ruth-Ann felt - not heard - felt - something different in the woods. She slowed her pace.

Something was there.

When she started walking again, she moved slowly, cautiously, a new edge to her awareness.

Ah.

Ahead of her. A large tree. Something was behind it.

Movement froze her. She felt her heart in her mouth.

Someone stepped out from behind the tree.

Tall.

Upright.

A woman.

Persephone. Sweat flowed down Ruth-Ann like waters.

She smiled. "Girl, you liked to scared me to death," she said.

Persephone approached gracefully. "I could tell you knew I was there," she said.

They hugged, dampness sticking them together for an instant.

"You got some Indian in you, don't you," asked Persephone.

"Choctaw."

"Mmhmm. White, too."

"Yes," said Ruth-Ann, "I don't know what. Maybe English."

Persephone nodded. "Come on, I'll walk with you. I've got about a mile more to go on this track."

"Good," said Ruth-Ann. "Company is good. We can even shoo the bugs off each other."

They both laughed.

The trail was too narrow for them to go abreast, so Persephone went ahead. She talked over her shoulder.

"Yes, I figured some Indian and maybe some white. That helps me judge what the African is in you. That - and where you're from. Around Mandarin, right?"

"Yes."

"Out there in the country - outside, really outside of Mandarin?"

"Yes."

"Well, I'd say for sure ... the African in you ... is Yoruba. Yoruba and Fon. Maybe ... maybe something else, too. But for sure - Yoruba and Fon."

"How can you know that, Persephone?"

"Because that's what I study. Like Mama Ona knows whether a baby will be a boy or a girl or born with a cowl. She

162

studies it. Tims and Solders know where to find bear, deer, and panther - any time of year. Because they study it. I study us. Africans. Most people don't know anything about Africans. They don't know an African is not just an African. They don't know that the people dragged over here didn't call themselves Africans. They had their own names for themselves - many different names. An African is somebody specific - Yoruba, Fon, Fulani. People think they were all the same - looked the same, talked the same, worshiped the same. I know better. Because. I study us.

"Africans can tell, by looking, where each other come from. So can I. It's harder telling the people who were born here. Everything's all mixed up here. Hausa with Ashante, Igbo with Wolof. Everything's all mixed up. And on top of that folks are mixed up with Indians, white people. It's much harder to tell what is the African in somebody born here. But if you got an idea - like where people brought to this part of Florida came from in Africa - and you see some traces that confirm that, then you've got the basis for an educated guess. And my educated guess for you Ruth-Ann is you got some Yoruba in you, and Fon. That's going to mix just fine with the Fulani in that little baby you're carrying."

Ruth-Ann wondered how it was that somebody in Stephen's family was always telling her more about her own self than *she* knew.

She filled her letters to her friends in Jacksonville with stories about the strange and wonderful people whose family she had joined.

Her depictions delighted Lavinia because they captured so fully what she herself had thought and speculated about those Wenders.

# 37

Mama Ona squatted by the bed and moved her hands and fingers all over Ruth-Ann's distended belly.

Ruth-Ann felt desperate.

I've got to say something before she blurts it out.

Mama Ona leaned over and put her ear to Ruth-Ann's "live" womb.

Mama Ona's eyes were closed. All of her attention was focused on listening. "Mmm. Mm-hmm," she murmured.

Mama Ona lifted her head up.

"Mama Ona, I don't want to know what my baby is."

"What?"

"I don't want you to tell me what my baby is?"

"Don't nobody have t'tell you what yo` baby is. You knows it good as anybody else. This here baby's a Wenders."

"I don't mean that. I don't want to know if it's a boy or a girl."

Mama Ona looked startled. "Child, why would you say a thing like that?"

"Because I don't want to know."

Mama took her hands off Ruth-Ann. She stood up. She was a tall woman.

"I ain't never heard sech," she said. "Why don't you want to know?"

Ruth-Ann lifted her head so she could look at her mother-in-law.

"Mama ... Mama Ona ... I ... I just want it to be a mystery."

"Child, it is. Havin` a child ain't nothin` but a mystery."

"You're right," Ruth-Ann turned away. Her back was to Mama Ona. "But I want it t'stay a mystery 'till my baby is born."

Mama Ona looked at the girl. She bent over and patted her on the forehead. "I understand mysteries," she said. "If you want to keep it a mystery, I will." She smiled.

"Thank you, Mama Ona."

She was hesitant to say more. She hadn't guessed Mama Ona would agree. She had been prepared for a fight. But despite her victory, she had more to say. Now, with the seconds slipping by, it was going to be hard to get the words out.

"Mama Ona?"

"Yes?"

The matriarch had already made a concession. She was not ready for the girl to initiate any further conversation.

Ruth-Ann heard it in her voice.

She plunged on anyway.

"Mama Ona. It's ... it's not just me. No one. No one can know, but you."

"What!"

"Nobody ... nobody else would be able to keep it a secret. I'd find out."

She lowered her eyes. She'd said as much as she could. She could carry her challenge no further.

Mama Ona realized Ruth-Ann was right. There was no way any of her children could keep such a secret. But the girl was so bold - to ask something like that of her.

"We'll see," she said. She turned and walked to the door.

165

## 38

Working in the North during the summer had never been hard for Stephen. He had delighted in it. It was an escape from the ubiquitous oppression of the South. He'd dreaded his return to Florida every November.

This year was different. Neither his mind nor his heart had returned to Massachusetts with his body. He enjoyed seeing his old friends, but he felt an incompleteness. All he could do was *tell* them about his bride. They could not see her. They could not meet her. They could not *know* his "better half."

The pleasures he could partake of that the greater freedoms the North afforded him, his favorite parks, the swells of the Atlantic along the coast, the rich deciduous forests, the wooded hill country, were all diluted. She was not there to share them. He would only be able to tell her about them. She could not taste them, see them, smell them. She could not be in possession of them, as he was. He did his best to put all of that into his letters, and he wrote her everyday. While he was writing, he felt connected to her, as if he were with her, talking to her. He felt the same way when he read her letters, which - like his - were delivered every day that somebody went to town. Still, he knew, try as he might, he could not capture the living experience as it would be, were they together.

The North, then, for Stephen, was alien from how he'd known it in the past. Now, it was pale, bland, deficit.

166

All of his feelings had been magnified when Ruth-Ann had written him that she was expecting their child. He had been shocked. Elated! He would be a father. The exuberance of the discovery elevated him to unexpected realms of delight. Too quickly these episodes were followed by periods of deepest anguish. He should be there, with her, and their child. He should be there for the first quickenings of the baby in her womb. He should be there to watch her belly grow and kiss its rounded contours. This was something he had not anticipated at all, and he wondered at the feebleness of his imagination. Why hadn't he foreseen this possibility? He could not even guess. As the weeks, then, months progressed, his longings deepened. Until, mid September, they changed - to anticipation, impatience, excitement. He would soon be returning home, to his own.

*

The baby came in late January, born the same month as Ruth-Ann. Stephen was home. Jenina and Persephone helped Mama Ona with the birth. A boy, his parents named him Stephen. Everyone loved him. Fat and healthy, he was the family delight. There were no complications with the delivery.

"That girl's a strong, healthy somethin`," said Mama Ona.

"You dropped him easy as passin` wind," she laughed. "You gon` have plenty more babies."

Unlike many of his contemporaries, Stephen had held no preference for the gender of his child. He knew that, eventually, given the healthy number of his siblings, there would be plenty of opportunities to pass on the family name. He never expected to be a patriarch on the scale of his father, to reproduce himself in an effort to populate his vast acreage. He had no such designs for his lineage. He was interested in how he and Ruth-Ann would build their own little family - and not in the South, in the North. There, the kind of man he was, could have more possibilities. That was the place where he wanted to bring his help-mate and their offspring. But all those were thoughts for his future, their future. For the present, he basked in the glow of being a father for the first time. He was glad to have a boy. He would have been equally glad to have a girl. What he had, most of all, was a little someone, who made of the three of them, a special set of people, whose fates were inextricably bound.

When Stephen left for the North in April there was another loaf in the oven.

## 39

The little boy learned to walk and talk early. He was doing both when his father came home in November. Ruth-Ann's belly was big and round with the new one on the way.

The first night Stephen returned, he turned on his side and raised up to look down at his wife. He couldn't see her. It was so dark in the room he couldn't see anything. But he could tell where she was and she could tell where he was.

"I've got some news," he said.

She grew alert in the dark. She could feel his breathing. She tried to take it into herself.

"What is it?"

"The Northrups lost their cook. They asked me to recommend someone."

"Oh," she said, "that's quite a compliment. They must think very highly of you, Stephen Wenders, the first." She giggled.

"Ruth-Ann, that's not why I'm telling you this." He paused again. He waited for her to ask why. When she didn't, he could hold it in no longer. "I - I want you to do it. We - we could work together. That way we could be together all year round."

She felt a skip in her heartbeat.

169

She had never dreamed of such.

"Can we take the babies? Will they let our babies be there with us?"

"I don't know. I didn't ask them. I didn't tell them I was thinking about you. I had to ask you first ... and Mama."

"Mama Ona?"

"Yes."

"Why do you have to ask Mama Ona?"

"Because. I. I didn't ask. But. I thought about it. And. And I don't think they'll let us bring the babies. I don't know of any help who have ever had babies on the Northrup's place. Children neither. They have a nanny for their own. And ... and if we can't bring the children, Mama Ona would have to agree to watch them. So, if you decide to come, and they won't let us bring the babies, Mama Ona would have to agree to take care of them."

She sat up so fast she almost bumped into Stephen's head. Only the swiftness of his reflexes saved him.

"Stephen, I can't leave my babies!"

"If Mama Ona takes care of them, it would still be family. It would be alright. She's a good mother. And we will be with them half a year."

"They're my babies - not Mama Ona's!"

"I know. I know. I didn't say it would be easy."

He reached forward and pulled her into him.

She was shaking her head.

He patted her on the back as he held her.

"Listen ... listen," he said.

"Listen ... listen ...."

When she stopped shaking her head, he said, "I know it would be hard. I know it would be hard. But I want you to think

170

about something. Mama Ona would be good. She would be good. And every year I'm away from *everybody* - you, the babies - *everybody*. This way, this way, at least we'd have each other. Nobody will be all alone. And half the year we'd all be together. The babies will know who their real mother is. And while we're away, we'll both be earning money - be able to save something for ourselves and our children - give them a future."

She didn't say anything. She held tightly to her husband.

*

The second baby, a daughter, looked like Ruth-Ann, everybody said. They named her Virginia. From the first she was always serious. She had a good sense of humor, but from a little baby she was always serious, purposeful. It seemed as if she were born knowing what she could do and it didn't take long for her to take responsibility for her older brother.

That spring, after Virginia was born, another January baby, there was a big decision to make. Who would go North in April?

171

## 40

It was better to park the automobile on the main road. He could always wash off the dust thrown on it by a passing vehicle. The scratches and scrapes left by branches and twigs on the bootlegger's rough trail was another matter. Walking the mile would let him stretch his legs.

He liked to walk. He took off his hat and held it in his left hand. He didn't want it knocked off his head and his right hand was occupied with an empty jug, his pointer finger hooked through the ring. He didn't mind the bugs the way Ruth-Ann did, or even the humidity. There were bugs and humidity in the North woods, too - just not the same summer heat.

The boy who stepped out onto the track from the bush was the camp sentinel. His name was Tootie. He was one of Jack Maple's sons. Jack ran the still. Stephen waved at Tootie. Tootie smiled and waved back. Since he had recognized Stephen instantly, he had not bothered even to raise the shotgun.

"How'dee, Mr. Wenders."

"Just fine, Tootie. How're you?"

"Fine, sir. Thankee."

"How's the cookin' goin?"

Tootie grinned. "Oh, we got a fine batch, Mr. Wenders. Gon' make yo' ol' jug sang."

Stephen laughed. "Well, if it's that good, I think I'll be doin`
my own share o` singin', too."

They both laughed.

Stephen kept on up the track.

At the still, along with his daughter, Betty-Lou, who served
as his chief assistant, Jack was busy filling jugs for his regulars.

He looked up as Stephen approached.

"Well, if it ain't old Stephen, back from the North."

Betty-Lou jerked up her head. A dazzling smile took over
her face when she saw Stephen.

"Morning, Jack," said Stephen, "you, too, Miss Betty."

"I see you brought yo` jug," said Jack. "Betty-Lou, take care
o` Stephen's jug."

He reached over and took Stephen's jug. He handed it to his
daughter who had run over to join them.

She made eyes at Stephen as she took the jug from her father.

Jack stood a barrel on its end. "Sit down, sit down," he said,
pointing to the barrel. "I know you jest came hikin` up that piece
from the road. Take the load off."

"Thank you, sir."

Stephen sat down on the barrel.

"Aah, that feels good."

Jack turned another barrel on its end and sat down beside
Stephen.

"Yessuh,' he said. "Feel good t'me, too.

"Tell me some mo` bout that up North," said Jack. "What
them Yankees is like."

"Like white folks," said Stephen.

They both laughed. So did Betty-Lou, standing by the still.

"Ain't no diffrunt from folks down heah," asked Jack.

173

Stephen cocked his head to think.

"Well, there are some differences. They are not as used to Colored, so ... they don't have a set way of acting. It's more like they don't know how to act. So, I guess that way, it's harder to know what they think. And because the laws are different, they can't quite *expect* us to behave in a certain way."

Betty-Lou walked up to the two men. She extended Stephen's jug with both hands. She kept her eyes fixed on his.

"I filled yo` jug with the bestest tastins, Mr. Wenders," she said. "Jest for you."

"Well, thank you, Betty," said Stephen as he reached out and took the jug from her hands. He smiled at her.

She lowered her head and stepped over to stand beside her father. She raised her eyes back to Stephen's.

"Stephen," said Jack, "I think Miss Betty-Lou would like to do a little spoonin` with you."

Betty-Lou blushed. But nothing in her face or body language contradicted her father.

"Well, Miss Betty," said Stephen, "I don't know if ol` Jack is puttin` me on - but if I wasn't a married man ...."

"That don't make no diffrunce," she said softly.

Jack laughed. "I don't know how's Miss Ruth-Ann would agree with that," he said. "Don't mind this gal. She jest at that age where she's feelin` womanish - and all these men comes out t` the still carryin` on about her, three-quarters of 'em married, too, and a whole passel old enough t` be her grand pappie. Her head's just in a whirl all the time."

Stephen smiled. He stood up, reached in his pocket and pulled out some folding money. He counted out the correct sum and handed it to Mr. Maples. "Mighty obliged, Jack," he said.

174

"You welcome," said Jack. He pointed to the barrel where Stephen had been sitting.

"You don't need t'be in no rush. Tell me mo` `bout them Yankees."

They both sat back down.

"Well, like I said, they're white folks. They definitely believe that the Negro has his place. It's just that they're not so sure where that is. They know it's below the white man, but just how much below ... they don't know.

"That means a shrewd Colored man, who has studied them, can make a way for himself."

"And, and ... is the white woman still out of bounds?"

They both laughed uproariously.

Betty-Lou didn't laugh. She was very attentive to how Stephen would answer.

"Yes. Yes, she is," said Stephen. "But when it does happen - and it happens there just like it happens here - it's not a killing crime. And I have seen a couple of Negroes legally married to white women."

"Well, I'll be damned."

"But that's unusual. I mean, it's very unusual."

"Still. That got t` be a diffrunt world."

"In some ways it is. And. And it's partly because of the Negroes. *They* act different. I wouldn't say it's whites so much, but the Negroes who act different. They won't put up with as much."

"Why you think that is?"

" I don't know - except I guess most of `em left the South to get away from that stuff, and they don't want to accept it outside the South. I don't know."

Jack leaned back. "You know, the Black man used to be in

175

the big-time right here in Jacksonville. Reconstruction."

Stephen nodded. "I've heard tell."

"That's right, Colored nearly 'bout ran Jacksonville. Better. It were better than it sound like that up North is right now. Big businessmen, Postmaster general. Government. Judges. Polices. Black people ridin' 'roun' in carriages with fancy drivers. Yessir."

"Times have changed."

"They has. I ain't tellin' 'bout what I heard. I'm talkin' 'bout my own pappy. He owned a line o' ferry boats. Sat on the city council. Had a house in town and a house in the country on the St. Johns. Life was sweet for the Colored man in Jacksonville. Reconstruction."

"What happened?"

"The crackas went crazy. Couldn't take it no more. Negroes lordin' it over 'em, payin' them wages. Makin' the rules. They went crazy. And that's how we got t' where we is now."

Stephen remembered Mr. Northrup's car parked off the main road. He stood up.

Betty-Lou moved so he could see her lush body pressing against the light fabric of her dress.

"I'm afraid," said Jack, "you gon' go up North one of these times and not come back."

"Maybe," said Stephen, "but I never heard tell you were much of a prophet."

They all laughed.

"Bye, Miss Betty."

"Bye, Mr. Wenders. Remember ... I always saves the bestest for you." She turned and ran back to the still.

176

# 41

Though Ruth-Ann did not want to be separated from Stephen again, going North was not something she had reconciled herself to. She had no desire to leave the only world she knew. She loved the Wenders. Her own family, too, was not far. She loved them. She needed them. She knew no one in the North. Stephen had told her about the cold. She was afraid of it, and the snow.

They sat on the step outside the door to her room - their room. Across the clearing from the house the woods rose, dense and green.

"You haven't made up your mind, have you," he asked.

"Stephen ...."

He looked at her.

"I'm not as old as you are."

He smiled softly and ran his hand over the top of her head.

"I know I robbed the cradle. And I'm glad I did."

A dimple creased her cheek.

"I don't have the experience you do. I haven't been anywhere. I don't know the world."

"I didn't either - until I went."

"I'm afraid."

He now was silent. What could he say against her fear? It was right to be afraid. Fear of the unknown. He also knew that was not all there was. She did not want to leave the children. As she should not. What kind of mother would she be if she *wanted* to leave them? If the decision were *not* excruciating?

He shook his head.

He turned to what he knew.

"You want me to stay here, don't you?"

Her face lit up and she turned it up to him.

"I know." He put his arm around her shoulders. "I wish I could. But I can't."

With his other hand he stroked her neck.

"Think about Calter. Think. About why you're living in the woods with my family. I cannot. I can't *stay* here. I can't live here. I can return. I can visit. But I can't *live* here."

She understood. Crazy as he was, it was better that he not stay. But what about her? Why should her husband be torn out of her life again and again? Either Stephen torn out - over and over - or her children. Any of it was too much to bear.

"Tell me," she said. "Tell me again about the North."

\*

Stephen did not know the man's name, but once in a great while he saw him in Jacksonville. He did not know his name, but he knew who he was.

A derelict. A bum. A wino. He was the one who had led the mob to break down Feemstead's back door and snatch Stephen out of the store. Every time Stephen saw him he felt paralyzed, constricted with fear. He lost even the ability to think. It was as if he turned to stone.

This was something he could never tell Ruth-Ann.

178

Some things you have to bear alone.

Why can't I live here? That's why. Because *staying* here does not mean *living* here. They have the prerogative - even the most wretched of them - to take my life on a whim. Then what am I to Ruth-Ann, to my children?

Always less than a man. Seeing the man was a reminder of those he did not see, or who upon seeing them did not recognize, yet who were always present about him. Ruth-Ann might mistake me, he thought. I do not love the North. But oh how I hate the South - and how I fear it. Unless you can isolate yourself as I have seen some do. Look at Jack Maples. Look at Papa. But unless you can do that - it is no place for a colored man to be a man.

As for a colored woman - the way Betty-Lou looked when her father asked about colored men and white women - she feared it would be true. Because here a colored woman is not seen as a *woman*. The only *woman* is white. A colored woman is female. She has the gender. She can arouse animal lusts. She can bear children - lord, of many colors. But she is not a *woman* - due the respect and adoration of a *woman*. No. She is an auntie, a mammy, hard, a *loose* woman, a subordinate - demeaned rather than esteemed. She is not and cannot be a *woman* because she is not and cannot be a *lady*.

# 42

Stephen was putting the finishing touches on polishing the Northrup's limousine one Saturday afternoon, when Wendell Hawkins came rumbling down the driveway, a grin plastered across his face. Stephen looked up, then straightened up. He dropped the rag across the hood and brushed off his hands.

"Wendell - what brings you across the street to see me? The Clarks don't have enough to keep you busy?"

Wendell didn't say anything. His grin just got bigger and he wagged his head from side to side.

"You just gon' stand there, Wendell, grab a rag and help me finish up."

Wendell didn't take a step, he just stood grinning and wagging his head.

"Got a message for you," he said at last. This time the grin popped his mouth wide open.

Stephen stared at him. Wendell was a fool. "Well ...."

"Message from a gal." Wendell didn't take a step. But he was moving and twitching so much in one place he looked as if he had an irresistible urge either to dance or have a fit.

Stephen waited.

"Don'tcha wanta know what it is and who it's from?" Wendell rolled his eyes.

What Stephen wanted was to grab the clown and pop him in his mouth. "I'm waiting," he said.

"Gal say," and at this Wendell started giggling almost uncontrollably," she want you t'meet her down at Posey's tonight." He squeaked out, at last, between giggles, "Round Midnight."

Stephen turned back to the limousine and picked up his rag. He turned his attention to the details he needed to put a flourish on. "Tell the lady," he said over his shoulder, "two things - number one, I'm busy this evening or I wouldn't even be in Jacksonville; number two, I'm a married man and that's the end of that."

Wendell took two hesitant steps forward.

"Don't you even want to know who she is?"

"Is she Ruth-Ann?"

"What?"

"Is she Ruth-Ann?'

"No -"

"Then I don't need to know and don't want to know."

Wendell started backing down the driveway, peeved.

"Well, I'm `on tell you, I'm `on tell you anyhow. It's Betty-Lou, Betty-Lou Maples! Ought t` be `shamed! Ought t` be shamed of yoself - leadin` on a *fine* young gal like that!"

Stephen stopped his work and looked up. "Gawn, gawn, Wendell! You did your job. You delivered your message!"

When Wendell disappeared, Stephen shook his head.

That woman is out of control.

181

# 43

Stephen parked the Northrup's limousine in the clearing. The walk wasn't much over two miles, still he was glad it wasn't raining. He got out of the car, locked it, and turned to the cart-track. Standing there was Ruth-Ann. He let out a whoop and dashed across the space separating them.

They embraced long and hard. He kissed her all over her face.

She leaned back and said, "I couldn't wait any longer - and I thought how wonderful it would be to walk back the whole way together."

He hugged her tightly. "One of the best ideas your pretty little head ever had."

She laughed.

They went to holding hands and started up the track. They talked for a long time about what they had been doing and who they had seen. Then, Ruth-Ann said, "Stephen. You know I love your people. Now, they're my people, too. Our children and me are all part of the family."

"I know that my angel."

"You still read your bible, Mr. Wenders?"

"Yes, Ma'am."

"The *Book of Ruth*?"

His eyes widened.

"Whither thou goest I will go," she said. "Whither thou lodgest, I will lodge. Thy people shall be my people, and thy God, My God."

*Springtime in the North* 1919

## 44

Stephen and Ruth-Ann drove North in the limousine. Mr. Northrup needed the car in Massachusetts, so Stephen drove it there a week ahead. When the Northrups came, they would travel by train. Stephen would meet them at the station.

Stephen and Ruth-Ann arrived at twilight. By the time they unloaded the car, it was dark. Ruth-Ann met the housekeeper, Claudette, and a groundsman, Sterling, both Negroes. Ruth-Ann spent the rest of the evening familiarizing herself with the house and kitchen.

During the night, snow fell. When Ruth-Ann awoke, raised the shade, and opened the curtains, she was terrified. She had never seen anything like it. The whole world was white, grey, and black. She wondered, for a while, if she were dreaming. The world, she told herself, does not look like this. I must be dreaming. I am asleep. She turned her back to the window so that she was looking into the room. She saw the ruffled bed clothes she'd taken so much time and care selecting the night before. Stephen lay asleep, his back to her. She turned back to the window. Outside, there was ... snow.

White. She'd known it was white. But when she'd imagined it, she'd pictured it as white on top of the green of Florida. Nothing had prepared her for the scene before her. There was no green.

There were no leaves on the trees. The ground was completely white. The trunks and limbs of the trees were black - black and grey. The sky was grey. The world - the whole world - had changed. It was not a world she knew. It was beautiful - beautiful - but alien. Terrifying. She gasped. The North was, it really was, *another world.*

She pulled the shade. She could not bear to look. She returned to bed and cuddled up to Stephen's back. She pressed herself close to him. He grunted in contentment. That calmed her a bit, but she wondered how he could sleep, knowing what was outside.

Two days later when the sun came out, the sky was the deepest, clearest blue she'd ever seen. The sunlight danced off the snow, the dazzling brilliance sparkling against the lapis lazuli of the heavens. The sight was astounding and coupled with cold such as she'd never imagined. This other world was hers. Her world now.

A week after the Northrups arrived, the snow melted. Buds began to appear.

Stephen was eager to show his wife Massachusetts. He'd planned that they'd spend the first week, - before they had to do any real work - seeing the sights. That's before the snow had paralyzed her - absolutely paralyzed her. He had never seen the like. He couldn't get over how such a brave young woman could let something as harmless as a snowflake immobilize her. But it did. So they spent that whole first week inside the Northrup house. She practiced the Northrups' favorite recipes. It worked out well. The Northrups were delighted with her from the very first meal served from her kitchen.

## 45

Stephen had the responsibility to introduce Ruth-Ann to the other Colored help in the area. Colored people usually got together for a social event at a public place on Thursdays. The place shifted around. It could be the seashore one week, a carnival the next, an amusement park sometime later, or a Colored restaurant or boarding house that served non-boarders. It took several Thursdays for her to meet everyone. Within seven weeks she had met all the people who would constitute her social life. They were friendly, welcoming, and easy to be around. They took to Ruth-Ann right away.

She took to them as well, the women more than the men, as she spent more time with the ladies. Her favorite among all her new acquaintances was Molly-Bell, just about the same age, and herself recently married. Her husband, James, was younger than Stephen, but that was almost the only appreciable difference between the couples, as James was a chauffeur, like Stephen, and Molly-Bell a cook, like Ruth-Ann. Like the Wenders, Molly-Bell and James had two children who were kept in the South, by their people.

Molly-Bell had been working summers in New England for several years, and took it upon herself to take Ruth-Ann under her wing and show her the sights. Often the two couples went places together, but now and again, the two young women went out on their own. Their husbands, as chauffeurs, were more at the beck and call

185

of their employers.

As she went about her daily work, or on excursions with Stephen, and with their friends, Ruth-Ann could not explain it, but especially as the season moved into late spring and early summer, she felt hemmed in. She could not put her finger on it until the day they finally made their way to Cape Cod, and before her stretched the boundless Atlantic. She relaxed, tension sliding off her shoulders.

In a flash, she knew what had afflicted her - claustrophobia. Everywhere she went, she was enclosed by trees, buildings, or both. All her life, the horizons had been open - even when obscured by a swamp or a forest-stand - it wasn't long before space opened up and reached out to infinity. Even Patterson's dense woods had been bordered by the open bay. In New England, the forest was all-encompassing except when it was replaced by buildings. The only place to see the blue expanse of the sky was to look up, above the tops of trees or steeples.

Once she realized why she had felt caged, and that relief was available, she not only felt more at ease, she began to appreciate the beauty of the Northeast.

*

There was more, however, than the natural and constructed worlds Ruth-Ann had to adjust to. There was also the Northrup household. The Northrups themselves, though they were the masters of the house, were not the principal features of Ruth-Ann's daily life. Her relationships with the Northrups were, for all intents and purposes, decidedly superficial. In addition to Stephen, the other people she really had to live with, were the other household servants,

186

and among them, there was a complex and multi-dimensional hierarchy. Her place in it was ambiguous.

The hierarchy was rooted in age, gender, length of tenure, and place. On three axes - Ruth-Ann's placement as a teenager, female, and most recently hired, was obvious. She was on the bottom. On the other hand, her position - cook - required respect. The household's daily schedule not only was structured around her work, what came out of her kitchen set the tone for the day, evening, weekends, whole seasons. Additionally, she directly supervised another worker - Quinteen, the scullery maid - and could bring others under her authority when the need arose, as with holidays, parties, and various celebrations.

If that weren't enough, everything was further complicated by individual personalities, the personal relationships among the servants, and the relationships of particular members of the staff with specific members of the Northrup family. In some households, these matters were further compounded by the impact of race. In the Northrup household, where all the help were Negroes, that particular difficulty did not arise. Yet Ruth-Ann's marriage to Stephen, the chauffeur - a position of responsibility and privilege - and a man who was highly esteemed by all the servants and the Northrups as well, mitigated in her favor, undercutting her handicaps of age, gender, and short tenure.

In Massachusetts, the Northrup help consisted of Ambrose, the butler; Stephen, the chauffeur; Ruth-Ann, the cook; Claudette, the maid; Dipsy, the Nanny; Sterling and Calumet, the gardeners; Winchester, the groom; and the scullery maid, Quinteen. They all lived on the place.

Because Ruth-Ann had absolutely no pride of place, she navigated the tricky waters with boundless ease. She embraced her role as the lowest on the totem-pole and simply did not accept any deference that might be paid her because she was the cook. These characteristics endeared her to her co-workers. It didn't take long for them to say, "That's one smart girl."

There were times Ruth-Ann and Stephen could count on being alone together. One was the early-mornings before the household was up while she prepped for breakfast. Stephen sat in the kitchen with her and lent his unskilled hand to her direction. Another was in the late night when Quinteen had finished the dishes and retired. Then the couple got the kitchen ready for the next day's breakfast and went to their room upstairs in the back of the house. There were some Thursdays when they both had the day off, though often Stephen had to work on Thursdays because Mr. Northrup needed him to drive.

*

As close as Ruth-Ann and Molly-Bell rapidly became, it nevertheless took some time before Ruth-Ann confessed how terrified she had been by her first snow storm. Once she told the tale, Molly-Bell doubled over with laughter and made Ruth-Ann recite it all over again, probing for more details each time. At last, exhausted by the comedy, Molly-Bell said, "Oh, girl, you the Snow Queen." The name stuck.

The cook had to do the grocery shopping and Ruth-Ann had plenty of experience doing that with Nidi. Nothing, however, had prepared her for the Boston fish market. It was three weeks before she could shop there on her own. First she took Stephen, Ambrose, and Claudette along. Very quickly Molly-Bell joined them. Then

188

other colored women from their crowd came along. After a while, most of the other women dropped out, until only Molly-Bell and Stephen remained . Stephen had to go because he was the chauffeur and drove the purchases back to the estate. Molly-Bell went because she was such a close friend. By then Ruth-Ann was doing the shopping herself, her two hangers-on there for the company and to revel in the fish-market experience, smell be-damned. She had not mastered the market, but she was able to do it justice.

## 46

Unlike Stephen, James had been in the war. One Thursday as the two couples strolled across a bridge over the Charles River, on their way to Cambridge, they stopped and looked down from the bridge wall at the water. They could see quite a distance. Many boats dotted the river. Some people were out for a leisurely afternoon, rowing awhile, then drifting. Others raced, or practiced hard, rhythmic strokes as their light, slim crafts skimmed along the surface. There were a few sail boats.

James laughed. "Ah don't know why - it don't look nothin` like it - but right now the river remin` me of the Seine, in Paris."

Stephen looked over at him. "Maybe it's the mood," he said.

"Yessuh, that could be it." James looked down at the water directly below the bridge. "You know," he said, "befo` Ah went ovuh theah, Ah thought that up north, heah, was free. Ah didn't know. It ain't nothin` like free."

"It's free over there?" asked Ruth-Ann.

"For a colored man," said James.

"This is good enough fo` me," said Molly-Bell. "Bettah than Carolina - I'll tell you that."

"It is, it is," said James. "An` Ah used t'think it was free.

190

But it ain't."

"I've heard men say that before," said Stephen, "about Europe. I don't know as how they could explain what makes it different, though."

"Ah don't know as Ah can," said James. "But, say, ovuh heah - in Boston, or Cambridge - it ain't no signs, but you know what stores you can go in and which ones you cain't. You knows if you wants t` eat it's best if you can find a colored place. Sure it's establishments what will serve you, but if you's in a neighborhood what you don't know, you ain't likely t` take a chance at the first spot you sees. Mo` likely than not, you'll spy aroun` `till you sees a place where there's already some Colored up in theah. It ain't like that ovuh theah. You jest goes right on in t` any place you please."

"I cain't hardly imagine that," said Molly-Bell.

Ruth-Ann laughed. "No. It doesn't sound real."

"And," said James, "when you goes in, they catches yo` eye, they nods. If they speaks English they says, "Good afternoon, suh, or good evenin`, suh. They takes you to a table. They pulls out a chair for you."

"And these are white folks?" asked Ruth-Ann.

"White as yo` boss-man," said James.

Ruth-Ann shook her head. "You're right, Molly-Bell, I can't imagine it either."

"Heah, said James, "it ain't never no doubt. Wherever you goes, whatever you does, you is a Colored man. Theah, you's jest a man."

Stephen looked down the Charles as far as he could see.

*Just a man.* It was a thought he could not possess. He was, through the marrow of his bones, *a Colored man.*

191

"I think," he said, "I'm too old to understand."

"There was mens," said James, "what didn't come back."

"Stayed over there? I'm glad Stephen didn't go," Ruth-Ann looked up at her husband. "I want him right here with me."

Molly-Bell took James' hand. "I'm glad *you* came back," she said. "What would I do without you?"

Stephen smiled. "Well, this is the Charles River, not the Seine," then he gestured broadly, "and this certainly isn't Paris."

They all laughed.

"Let's go find us a place in Cambridge where we can eat."

They chuckled and resumed their stroll.

## 47

As long as the weather allowed, one of the favorite Thursday activities for Colored were picnics. They reminded Ruth-Ann of the Jacksonville Fourth of July picnic when she'd met Stephen. There were big differences - one was that in Boston there were lots of picnics, another was that in Boston there weren't nearly as many people in attendance. Unlike Jacksonville, in the Boston picnics, just about everybody knew each other, but as in Jacksonville, they all tried to outdo each other in the splendor of their meals. Sometimes the picnics were held on the banks of the Charles. Other times people piled onto trolleys and found a place in the country. Now and again they'd pack onto a bus headed for the Cape or the Vineyard. They were good times, alive with gaiety.

When the weather was right, on the trips to Cape Cod or Martha's Vineyard, the younger folk packed bathing suits. In the afternoon they'd change into them and play in the Atlantic. Some actually swam, but most waded and splashed in the waves. The older people sat on their blankets and watched.

One day when Ruth-Ann was first out of the water, she toweled herself dry, laid down on their blanket, and looked across the beach and out over the water. The conversation they'd had overlooking the Charles came back to her. It hit her that it was perfectly normal, and nobody thought it might be otherwise, that everybody she could see from her spot on the sand, was Colored. It never entered anyone's mind that a white person would be there. Several people appeared white, but everyone *knew* they were Negroes. So in her mind they were not white. Her eyes closed as her thoughts reached back to that day on the bridge. The four of them had been the only Negroes in sight. Everyone else had been white. Indeed, New England was overwhelmingly white and - unlike Florida - there were comparatively few Colored. Yet, no one took it as odd that this whole seascape was filled with Negroes without a white person in view. How odd that it was not odd. Before that day on the bridge, the incongruity of the situation would never have dawned on her. Lying there with her eyes closed, the voices within earshot all spoke in familiar tones and rhythms, her people.

# 48

Three full months passed before Ruth-Ann realized that when the Northrups and their help returned South, Sterling, Calumet, and Winchester would not come with them. She had never worked for the Northrups in the South. Stephen was the only member of the staff she had known before she came to Massachusetts. The revelation, which came from a conversation with Claudette, deeply puzzled her. That night as she lay beside Stephen, she asked him why the three men wouldn't be coming to Jacksonville.

"Sterling and Calumet stay here all year round because someone has to take care of the place during the winter. While you can rest assured there's no gardening, there's still plenty to do. You've seen for yourself that it snows. Someone has to keep the walks and driveways clear. Someone has to see to it that the roof doesn't get overloaded with snow or the gutters clogged up.

"Because of the danger of freezing and bursting pipes, the house and stables have to be kept warm. Winchester doesn't come South because the Northrups don't keep a stable in Jacksonville. They do all their riding while they're up here. So Winchester stays here to keep the horses fed, cared for, and exercised. When he can, he lends Sterling and Calumet a hand with their chores.  Also, with three grown men around all the time, it's unlikely that anybody would try to break into the place."

"But if both gardeners stay up here during the winter, what do they do for a gardener in Jacksonville?"

Stephen laughed.  "They use one gardener in Jacksonville, Toliver, and he's there year round.  See, the difference is, here, you actually have to *make* things grow.  There, you just control the growth.  It's going to grow - you just have to direct it, or stop it, before it goes wild.  Plus, the grounds are much bigger here.  Toliver is the caretaker there.  Here, they've got a total of three caretakers.  There, they have just the one."

"So, Stephen, is this the main house?"

"Yes.  I'd say that.  It's the biggest house.  It's the fanciest house.  They do more entertaining here,  you'll see the difference - and be glad for it - when we go back to Jacksonville.  Mr. Northrup's business is headquartered here.  They spend much more time here.  On the average, they spend seven and a half months here and four and a half in the South."

"And that's another reason you wanted me to come North with you?"

"Yes."

"Now.  What about the Northrup children?  If they're here seven and a half months and three of those months are in the summer, that leaves only four and a half months to go to school here.  If they have the Christmas holidays, only four months.  What do they do about that?"

"Well, up to now, they've had tutors.  The oldest one won't start school until the fall.  And that will be no problem.  He'll go to boarding school.  They'll all go to boarding school

196

when they come of age."

"Boarding school?"

"Yes. They'll live at the school and come home for the summers and holidays."

"Those little kids?"

"Yes. That's the way they do it."

"But I thought only Colored went to boarding school - like you, Stephen - and they only do it so they can go to high school. Because there are not enough Colored high schools."

"That's in the South. And that's for Colored. It's different here. Here there are plenty of schools for everybody. Everybody can go to school if they want - even Colored. Here they don't *have to* go to boarding school - for high school or anything else. There are enough public schools for everybody. The Northrups' children won't go to boarding school because they *have to*. They'll go because their parents *want them* to. People like the Northrups don't send their children to public schools. What would it look like, their children attending schools with Negroes and poor, white trash? They couldn't hold their heads up straight in the company they keep. That's why they don't send their children to the public schools - which are free. They send them to private schools - which are not free. They not only are not free, they are very expensive. That insures that only the right kind of children will be there. And they not only go to school there, they *live* there, with other little children, very much like themselves."

"But Stephen, the Northrups don't seem prejudiced. They're very nice to me - to us."

"They're no more prejudiced than anybody else, and a lot less prejudiced than most. I'm not really talking about prejudice.

197

I'm talking about how they live.

"Now, Ruth-Ann, think about it. All the personal staff - that's you, me, Ambrose, Claudette, Dipsy, and Quinteen - six people, travel with them wherever they go. A total of four people are on the place at all times - that's counting both here and in Jacksonville. That's ten people altogether. And each 'place' is a mansion, an estate. All these people - all of us, not only have to be paid - we have to be fed. The 'place' has to be big enough to hold separate living quarters for up to nine extra people. Both mansions have to be heated, the horses have to be fed, shoed, and taken to the veterinarian. I'm not talking about the basics for the Northrups themselves - food, clothing, recreation, transportation. Every now and then they sail across the ocean to Europe.

"I'm talking, Ruth-Ann, about how they live. The only way you can understand why Sterling, Calumet, and Winchester stay here in Massachusetts while the family and all the rest of us go South to Jacksonville, to be met by Toliver, is to understand how they live.

"Their world - in more ways than color - is not our world. We live - in part of their world. Our presence in part of their world makes the way they live possible. So while we're of their world, we're not in it."

Ruth-Ann knew she would have to spend more time on those numbers, and understanding what they meant. She also knew Stephen would be all too happy to help her understand. She smiled at the thought. But she wanted to put that matter aside for awhile. There was something else she had been wondering about.

"Why - Stephen - let me ask you something else. Why

... do they only have Colored help?"

"I don't know. I've thought about that myself, but I don't know. Some people have mixed help - some white, some colored. Some only have white help. Most of the people who do that have a lot of foreigners. I guess a lot more white people overseas do work like we do than here. I don't know. Then there's some, like the Northrups, who only hire Colored. A lot who do that are from the South. That's what they're used to. But the Northrups aren't from the South. So I don't know.

"But I have lately figured out something that's been a bit of a puzzle for me."

"Stephen, you are admitting that there's something in the whole, wide world that has puzzled that brilliant brain of yours?"

"Hush-up girl."

"Because you're trying to tell me something."

"That's right."

"I can read this old man's mind, say what's on it before he can."

Alright. Alright. If you're so smart, tell me what I'm about to say."

"I could! I could! But I'm too kind to take the wind out of your sails. You tell me, you tell me, Stephen, what you've figured out."

He paused.

But he could not refrain himself. He was proud of his accomplishment.

"Alright," he said. "I'll tell you, but don't think for a minute I believe you already know."

She laughed. "Go ahead. Tell me." She knew he wouldn't be able to resist.

199

"The reason," he said, "that they had us drive up before them, and they took the train - is so that you and I wouldn't have to take the jim-crow."

Ruth-Ann was still.

Then. "Stephen, do you really think they -"

"I do."

She was quiet again.

"Good people," she said.

"Good as can be expected."

## 49

Ruth-Ann and Stephen had developed their affinity for letter writing when Stephen's service in the North kept them apart.  While it took Ruth-Ann some time to accept the separation at all, once she accommodated herself to it, she became an enthusiastic and voluminous correspondent. They loved both to write and receive letters.  They would have found their correspondence much more fulfilling had they been writing each other, than they did  writing their friends and families.

Both wrote letters almost daily, Ruth-Ann a few more each week than Stephen. Some  evenings, after dinner, they sat in their little room together, each in another world, reaching out to some distant heart and mind.  Strangely enough, the effort brought them closer.

\*

"Stephen, you remember that day on the bridge?"

"Oh, there you go again, girl, always talking about that bridge.  It's as if you lived your whole life asleep and suddenly woke up on that bridge."

"I don't know about that, but I was just thinking about that bridge. You know how James said it reminded him of the Seine, but it didn't look like the Seine?"

"Yes, and I told him maybe it was the mood that did it."

"That's right, you did. Well, I've been thinking, how with all the boats out on it - that it reminds me of the St. Johns - though it doesn't look like it."

"Mmhmm. I can see that."

"And what else I've been thinking is that if it were the St. Johns, a lot of those people out in those boats would have been Colored, but everyone we saw that day was white."

"Mmhmm. That's right, too."

"Ever since that day I've been thinking that's something I'd like to do - go out for a boat ride on the Charles. Do you think we could do that? Do you think they would rent out a boat to Colored?"

Stephen leaned his head back. He was silent for a moment.

"Well, that's something to think about," he said. "That's something I'd like to do, too. I think it would be right pleasurable. But I don't know. I don't know if they'll rent to Colored. I'll make some inquiries."

Ruth-Ann brightened right up.

"Oh good! Thank you, Stephen. Thank you so much."

## 50

Sitting on the front seat of the rowboat, facing forward, Ruth-Ann beamed with happiness. She loved the way the boat felt as it moved over the water. She delighted in the sights - the water, the shore, the other boaters. She wanted to giggle, but all that happened was an irrepressible smile. She'd known Stephen could do it. She knew he'd be able to get a boat. He'd busied himself in his genteel way, "making inquiries," until he'd acquainted himself with a Negro who worked for the Fitches who told him of a white man he knew who would rent a boat to Colored. And here they were!

Stephen leaned back on the oars. He rowed so easily that the boat glided over the water. Staring at the back of the boat, while Ruth-Ann' sat at the front, and stared ahead, amused him. With a loud voice, he recited,

"Here's to good old Boston,
Land of the Cape and the cod,
Where the Cabots speak only to Lowells,
and the Lowells speak only to God."

Ruth-Ann whirled her head around. "Stephen Wenders, what are you palavering about?"

"I'm just trying to figure out which one you are - a Cabot or a Lowell."

"Stephen, I don't know what you're talking about."

He leaned back on the oars. "It just seemed to me - here I am a man hard at work, struggling with these big old oars, fighting the current, sweat popping off my face, and there you are, turned completely around, sitting with your back to me. You must be somebody high and mighty. So are you a Cabot or a Lowell, because between them and God, there's nobody else they speak to."

She blushed. She turned around in her seat. "I'm sorry Stephen," she said. I wasn't thinking. I'm just so excited. I'm so very thankful you did this for me. Here, let me move to the back, so we can look at each other."

"I love you my Snow Queen," he said.

She reached over the side and splashed water on him. "Don't' call me a Snow Queen! That's what Molly-Bell calls me - and she has her nerve!"

Stephen laughed. As his hands came up in the stroke, he wiped the water off his face. "I didn't call you a Snow Queen. I called you *my* Snow Queen."

That was the first time they went rowing on the Charles, but it was not the last. After awhile they got James and Molly-Bell, as well as others to join them. The man who rented boats to Colored got a lot more business than he expected.

## 51

Stephen couldn't understand why the car was shaking. Everything had been going perfectly, then he had shifted gears, and the car started shaking. He assumed it would stop, but it didn't. He took it out of that gear and put it in another. It kept shaking. This had never happened to him before. He couldn't understand what it was, but he couldn't stop driving. He couldn't stop driving and the car wouldn't stop shaking until he realized he was in bed.

Ruth-Ann's back was to his and she was shaking. He turned over. She was sobbing. He wrapped his arms around her, bringing her back against his chest. "What's wrong, little one, what's wrong?"

She held tightly to his hands, squeezing them, but her sobbing only worsened as she no longer tried to conceal it. Her body shook and shook.

He pressed his face into the back of her head.

"What is it my little one?"

Minutes passed before she could speak.

"Stephen, when we go home, my babies won't know me."

Her fingers dug into his hands.

He freed one of his hands and stroked her shoulder.

"We will have been away from them for seven and a half months," she said, "seven and a half months! And we will only get to stay with them four and a half months - four and a half months! Stephen, my own babies won't know me - and each year it will be worse!"

Stephen held her tight with one hand and stroked her shoulder with the other. "I think you may be right about Virginia," he said. "But Stephen will. Stephen will know you. You ... are his heart. Year-to-year he will keep you with him - inside - as you keep him.

"And next year Virginia will remember you, too. And keep a place for her Mama inside. But this year, you are right. It will be very hard."

"Oh, how can I bear it," she asked. "I'm only a girl myself. And I'm pregnant."

\*

The fall came at last, early fall. It was a lot like summer except that the days were shorter and the nights longer. Fall was cooler in the mornings, cooler in the late evenings, but without the humidity of full summer. Ruth-Ann found it pleasant.

There was a quickening in her, too. A quickening because she knew the time that kept her away from her children was narrowing. She no longer experienced it as lengthening. And there was a quickening in her womb from the new life.

The Northrups took their first son to boarding school.

206

When they returned, Mrs. Northrup spent a lot of time crying. It was hard for her, too, to depart from her child. Mr. Northrup sympathized with his wife, but as for his son's absence, all he said about it was, "He's a trooper."

Molly-Bell's employer, the Bowtins, went away for a few days. Molly took the opportunity to stop by after lunch every day. She and Ruth-Ann talked about the weather.

"I like it when it's like this," said Molly-Bell. "I don't worry about the weather until the rain starts to get cold. Then I'm ready to get away from here.

"But you know what happens before that, don't you Ruth-Ann?"

"As many times and as many people as have told me, how could I not," said Ruth-Ann.

"The fall colors," they said in unison.

"But the reason why everybody says it, and the reason why everybody wants you to see them, is because it's true," said Molly-Bell.

"Beautiful," said Ruth-Ann.

"Spectacular," corrected Molly.

And they were.

*Winter 1920*

# 52

Ernest was a careful student of his oldest brother - not simply how he walked, talked, and dressed. He wanted to be like his brother not only on the outside, but on the inside as well. He'd find out what he was reading, and read that. Whenever he could, he hung around when Stephen was listening to the gramophone or radio. Those tastes became his.

He reasoned that if he became like Stephen on the inside, he could live life like Stephen even more surely than if he lived like him on the outside. His mastery of his brother's internal self was his hole card. It would not fail him as external appearance alone might.

A good deal of studying Stephen consisted of surveillance. Where did he go? What mode of transportation did he use? What did he do when he got there? Because Stephen was a chauffeur, he drove a lot. It was hard for Ernest to follow him when he did that. But he did his best. He used short cuts. Ernest had learned to drive and secured employment as a driver and a chauffeur, but he was not free to drive and follow Stephen wherever he went. He had to drive where his employers wanted him to. As a result, following Stephen when he drove was not feasible. But whenever he could, he watched Stephen drive, so he would be able to mimic him when he got behind the steering wheel. Despite Ernest's limitations, he was able to keep a reasonable handle on Stephen's comings and goings, including the occasional sojourn to hidden locations in the deep woods.

*

Tootie didn't even bother to come out of his hiding place. He just whistled at Ernest to let him know he was seen and waved him on. Ernest smiled. He continued on the trail exactly as he believed Stephen would have. *I wonder if Tootie knows it's me or if he thinks I'm Stephen.* He chuckled. *Who knows?*

Jack Maples knew.

"Good t` see you Ernest. I see's you gots yo` jug with you."

"Surely, I do, Mr. Maples."

"Papa, is that Ernest Wenders?"

That voice froze Ernest. He wouldn't have been surprised if his heart had stopped beating. He was afraid to look up. He certainly couldn't speak.

Suddenly there was no need to look up.

She was standing straight in front of him.

He was completely frozen.

He knew his heart had stopped beating.

He didn't care.

He wanted to scream.

Suddenly he was hot all over.

Sweat popped out of his head.

His joins jutted out in his trousers.

He knew what he felt was lust.

He felt it raging through his body.

Nobody had a body like Betty Lou.

The sight of it staggered him.

She was beautiful, too, with a smile that ripped across his heart.

Her voice was musical, as if she sang when she spoke.

Ernest felt his legs go weak.

He feared he was going to fall to his knees.

He looked for help to Mr. Maples.

Mr. Maples glanced at his daughter. "Girl, cain't you see who it is? Don't be askin' me no foolishness. Here! Fill up this boy's jug for him."

He slipped the jug from Ernest's sweaty grasp and handed it to Betty-Lou.

She switched off toward a giant cask. Calling over her shoulder, she said, "Ernest come with me, you know I cain't do this by myself."

He stumbled after her like an automaton, not a thought in his head. She took the long way, going around a shed. When he turned the corner, he walked straight into her. His jug was on the ground. He felt the full softness of her body. Her arms were coming up over his shoulders. He felt her breath. Its fragrance ached in his chest. She was opening her mouth. Finally he did scream with his whole body, but nobody heard it. Her mouth had closed over his.

210

# 53

Ruth Ann's and Stephen's third child and second girl was born in mid-winter, another January baby. They named her Wynfried, after Papa's sister-in-law. Once she got past her new-born redness, her color was dark, like Stephen's and Stephen Jr.'s, and unlike Virginia's. Wynfried loved attention. She would do almost anything to get or hold somebody's attention, even cry if she had to. But she loved to play and loved it even more if somebody was watching her.

Mama Ona told Ruth-Ann, "I told you, you was gon` have a easy time passin` babies. Girl, you were born to have children. You gon` have a whole tribe o` children. Every time you comes here for the winter, you drops a new one. Some pretty little babies, too."

Ruth-Ann smiled at her mother-in-law. "Don't put all the burden for giving you grandchildren on me. You can't fool me, Mama Ona. You're the one who wants me to keep on having these babies. But you can't rely on me to go on and produce all your grandchildren - and you wouldn't have to - if you let some of your own children get married and have children of their own."

"Ruth-Ann, what in the world is you talking about? If my children had some judgement about who they went steppin` out with - the way Stephen did - they could have been done married a long time ago."

Stephen heard the conversation and cut in, "And pigs could fly, Mama. Pigs could fly."

He and Ruth-Ann looked over at each other and burst out

211

laughing.

Persephone listened to the exchange and shook her head "This is just what Mama wants," she said, "to make a typical winter just like this one, and like every other winter since Stephen and Ruth-Ann got married. When Ruth-Ann comes home, Mama gets another grandchild. That's it, winter means Ruth-Ann coming home, and having another baby."

"How I wish it was me," said Jenina. "How I wish it was me."

# 54

The railing on one of the many porches that festooned his father's house made a convenient perch for Stephen as he stared off into the woods that led to the St. Johns. He knew his father was somewhere off in there. Stephen had been thinking for months and mulling over in his mind much longer than that - for years - what he wanted to say. Now was the time. All he had to do was get his butt off the railing and traipse into those woods until he found the old man. But doing it was more than a notion. He chewed on a piece of dry grass. He glanced around the house. No one was about that he could make small talk with. *No*, he thought, *everything points to it. Now is the time.* He slid off the rail and paced deliberately across the field that led into the timber.

As well as he knew the forest, even with a good notion of where he might find his father, it took a long while before he saw him. He should have known Tattler would be with him. The old man loved that dog. And the dog loved the old man. Tattler's long body, belly down, stretched out over the ground. He watched the man work. The Wenders patriarch was setting crab traps along the edge of a slough. Stephen smiled. His father loved water.

He experienced a sudden epiphany. That love of water

had led the man, as a youth, to go on the high seas as a way of raising the bride-price for his beloved. Many young men of the time had gone on the road with the Pullman cars to make their fortunes. But not Papa Wenders. The road was not the way for him - his was the bounding main.

Stephen stepped forward. Whether it was sound or motion, the dog alerted to him. The large animal fixed his attention on Stephen. As the man moved forward, the dog tensed. When he recognized who the approaching figure was, Tattler sprang to his feet and trotted toward him, bobbing his head and wagging his tail. The dog's motion caught Mr. Wenders' attention.

"Boy! You come all the ways out here t'steal my dog?"

Tattler reached Stephen. The young man bent over and scratched his head. "No, sir," he called back." I came out here to see my father."

"My, my, my," said Papa Wenders, "you must have somethin' heavy on yo' mine t' track me down way out heah."

Stephen kept walking, Tattler moved lightly beside him, occasionally glancing up.

"I suppose I do," said Stephen, reaching out his hand to his father. The older man grabbed it with his own - and gave it a short, powerful squeeze.

"Well, why don't you tell me about it while I finish settin' out these traps?"

He waited for his son's assent.

Stephen nodded.

Papa Wenders turned back to his work.

Tattler lay down between them.

It was easier, Stephen realized, to think about talking to his father than doing it. He paced, slowly, back and forth over a

214

short distance. He stopped and looked out across the slough.

"It's pretty out here, isn't it," he said.

His father stayed busy at his work.

"Boy, I know you didn't come all this way to tell me that."

"No. No, I didn't."

Stephen looked up at the sky, then to his father's back, bent over, hard at work.

"Papa I know you love this land.

"I know how hard you worked to get it, build it up, and maintain it as a legacy for our family.

"But I. I ... can never be a farmer."

Mr. Wenders burst out laughing. He stood up and held his sides. He kept on laughing.

When finally he finished, he said, "I hope that's not the big news you came way out through all them woods t'tell me. I know they say it's no fool like an old fool, but even I have never been a big enough fool to think I was goin` t` make a farmer out of you."

He started laughing again and couldn't stop.

Stephen watched him and, finally, smiled.

"I guess not," he said, "but that's the beginning of what I wanted to tell you." They both laughed.

"Alright, son," said Mr. Wenders, "why don't you get on to the hard part." He turned back to his labors.

"Papa," said Stephen, "I'm the oldest son, so a good part of this farm should be my inheritance."

"I ain't dead yet, boy!"

"I didn't -"

"So don't go buryin` me before my time!"

"No, sir."

"Alright, then, get on with it."

"Well, Papa," I been thinkin` on it a lot, and I don't think Ruth-Ann and me should be raising our children here - in the South. I'm not cut out for it. And ... and I don't want the children t` have to come up through it.

"You know what almost happened with Patterson. You know what they did to me over the typewriter. And I'm not going to have any homestead of my own t` keep all that away from my children. They're going to have to live right up in the middle of the horror, the terror, the degrading monstrosity of jim-crow."

Mr. Wenders stood up and turned to face his son.

"Those are hard words."

"I mean every one."

Mr. Wenders pointed to a giant log.

"Why don't we go sit over theah," he said.

Tattler watched the two men walk to the log and sit down. He didn't move his head. He followed them with his eyes.

"So do you mean t'tell me," said Mr. Wenders, "You're thinkin` about movin` up North - with your family - permanent?"

"Yessir."

"And what about us. Here in Florida? What are we supposed to do?"

"Sir?"

"Part of the family just git up and go. We're not whole anymore. What we s'posed t'do?"

"I - I -"

"Y'see, son," he looked over at his dog. "Tattler," he pointed over to the long, dark animal, "he ain't nothin` but a dog,

216

but I'd feel mighty badly if he decided t'get up and move on away from here."

"Yessir, but we ... can visit."

"Visit!"

"Yessir."

"You mean like the folks come out here t' get your mother's charms and potions? Like them folks what comes t' get Tims and Solders t' take 'em huntin' or fishin' - visit!"

"No, Papa, it wouldn't be like that. We're family."

"That's what I'm talkin' about. You're family. How you just gon' pick up and go?"

"I'm not talking about right away."

Mr. Wenders paused.

"Not.

"Not ... talkin' about right away?

"Then what you talkin' about?"

"The future."

"Future?"

"Yes, Papa. It's not like we could leave now. We don't have any place we could live in the North. Fact is, we'd have to get service work with people who lived there year round before we could move up there permanently. We can't do that now. We work for the Northrups and you know they spend every winter right here."

"That's what your Mama told me."

"She told you the truth. So we would have to get us another situation before we could even think about living up there year round."

"So, Stephen, you're just tellin' me about your plans."

"That's right, Papa. We plan. One day. To live in the

North."

"Hmm. I guess that means - Ernest, one day, will plan - to live in the North."

They both laughed.

"That son of yours."

"That brother of your'n."

"You know Ernest, Papa."

"Sure do. But don't tell your Mama."

They both broke out again.

"Oh, no," said Stephen through gales of laughter. "That would be the end."

"Of Ernest," added his father.

Tattler stared at the two. He didn't know what to make of them as they almost tumbled backwards off the log.

## 55

To Stephen, the talk with his father was his Rubicon. He was surprised that his Papa understood. As he thought back over it, he guessed it was because Papa had understood it as a plan, that Stephen took his life seriously enough, and the life of his growing family seriously enough, to plan for the future. And the plan was realistic. It was based on the way Stephen saw the possibilities for his life, and for theirs.

Afterward, Stephen came to the conclusion that he shouldn't have been surprised at all. Wasn't that what his father had done when he left Florida, stepped on a ship, and sailed away to the far reaches of the world? Negroes weren't doing that in those days, but his father had a plan.

Stephen had known his decision was the right one. He was willing to stand up to his father to defend it. But he found out he didn't have to, because his father was standing right there with him, side by side, man to man. Tears came to his eyes.

When he went back to the house to tell Ruth-Ann, she understood. She knew as he spoke, what she felt and why she felt it at the Monday market, when she'd seen him turn, like an eagle in the air, and knew he had to be her husband.

219

# 56

Jasper Hanks might have been a wino, an out-and-out inebriated, derelict, filthy, and incorrigible wino, but he had a memory for faces, even nigger faces - and one nigger face in particular. That was the face of the nigger who had the audacity and the impertinence to arrogate himself above white men by operating that infernal writing machine. He was the one they had the right and the responsibility to punish for that intolerable offense, and upon whom they had almost carried out righteous justice on behalf of the white race when he had been rescued by that shame-faced fool, Jason Wenders. Jasper never forgave Jason Wenders and he never forgot the nigger.

His alcoholic blood had become inflamed the first time he saw the nigger driving that big, black limousine, all decked up like somebody fancy in his chauffeur's uniform. First a writing machine, then a big, black limousine - and a chauffeur's uniform! It was insufferable. The nigger would pay the price, and this time he would not get away - Jason Wenders be damned.

Jasper Hanks had another characteristic. He was singularly persistent. That characteristic kept him alive, despite the sclerotic state of his body, and the rotted state of his brain. By tracking the limousine every time he spotted it and ceaselessly badgering people with obtuse questions , belching breath tainted by wine, whisky, and bad teeth, he was able to find out that the conceited nigger was Alfred Northrup's chauffeur.

All I have t'do now, thought Jasper, is set the trap for him, set the trap. Jasper's binges, sicknesses, and comas often rendered him so debilitated that he was incapable of focusing on the revenge he was hell-bent to visit on Stephen Wenders, but all it took was seeing the limousine again to renew his rage and fire his ambition.

\*

For the first time in his life, Ernest was not the least interested when Stephen came back from the North. The event barely registered with him. His whole being was devoted to slavish worship of Betty Lou Maples. He could think of nothing else and he wanted to think of nothing else. Day or night, sleeping or awake, his thoughts pursued her.

She made love to him and took him to such realms of ecstacy that he no longer dwelt on mortal earth. He lived in paradise.

It is unlikely that his consciousness of Stephen's presence in Jacksonville would have become active at all had the words not issued from Betty Lou's lips.

"Stephen's back in town, ain't he," she said.

"What?"

"Your brother, Stephen, he's back in town, ain't he?"

"Uh, yeah, I think so. I guess so."

"Ain't you happy?"

"Uh, no - I don't know. I guess so. Why?"

"Oh, I just heard he was. That's all."

What Betty Lou did not say, but felt, was that now that

221

she'd had one Wenders man, she'd proved she could do it. Now, maybe she could get another, the oldest one, the one she really wanted. She smiled as she hugged Ernest. He couldn't see her face, but something about the way she was holding him didn't feel right. Suddenly, out of nowhere, as if he had been struck by lightning, searing jealousy ripped through him.

*

The first time Jasper Hanks saw Ernest Wenders, he thought he was Stephen. But he was puzzled. He wasn't driving the Northrup limousine. He was driving the Washburn car. That puzzled Jasper. First he passed it off as the dt's. But another day he saw him driving someone else's car. When that happened, Jasper tried to stay sober long enough to figure it out, but he couldn't. He learned a few weeks later that Stephen wasn't even in town any more. He'd gone North with the Northrups. If that were the truth - and it seemed to be - who the hell was the nigger he'd seen driving all over town?

Jasper never did figure it out, but one day it just hit him that he'd seen the nigger before. He thought about it until he remembered he'd seen him out at Jack's still, hanging around Jack's daughter. Jasper had always aimed to get himself a piece of that one day so he was always envious of whatever young bucks he saw spoonin' her. Oh, yes, he wanted some o' that. It was too good to be wasted on niggers. But who was he - that nigger?

It was a long time before he heard he was Stephen Wenders' brother. When he did, he smiled his broken, snaggle-

222

toothed, brown-pitted grin. There had to be some way he could use that.

*

It took a long time, but time is one thing Jasper Hanks had plenty of. It took a long time, but he was finally able to find some of the men who had been involved in the aborted lynching of Stephen Wenders. He told them that being rescued had gone to the nigger's head, he was surer than ever that he stood head and shoulders above a white man. He told them about how he was now driving around in a big, black limousine, longest car you'd ever see. Next thing you knew, he'd have a white woman riding in there with him. He got so worked up he just let the spit fly. He also found a few men who hadn't been involved when the mob got Stephen, but who'd heard about it and were sorry they'd missed it. Jasper told them that if they'd get involved, they could see to it that it was done right and Jason Wenders be damned.

Trouble was, Jasper knew they couldn't just snatch the nigger off the street. He was always connected up with somebody important. This time it was Alfred Northrup. If anyone seen them snatch him out of Northrup's limousine, there'd be hell to pay. They had to catch him at night, alone somewhere, like they'd done before. That would be hard to do. The only time he was around Jacksonville he was in that limo and always driving Mr. Northrup or his family. No white person knew anywhere else to find him.

One of the new men said they ought to ambush the nigger. Well, that was all fine and good, but how was they

223

supposed to find him to ambush him? That's when Jasper recollected about the boy who he knew was the nigger's brother. There had to be some way they could use the boy to find and catch that high and mighty black bastard.

*

He saw the young nigger again, out at the still. Jasper wanted to kill him. He wanted to get his hands around his neck and strangle him. He was with that wench again. Jack's daughter, the one who was so much woman she was driving Jasper crazy. If that stupid boy hadn't been around, he could have got her off into the woods, drug her down, and give her some o' what she was born for. He wouldn't mind having a few mulattoes by the heifer. Maybe I'm gon' have t' kill both them niggers befo' it's over with because I'm gon' get me some o' that.

*

The men sat on the back steps of Dr. Swenson's house, waiting for his office hours to end. Then they could get on in there and start their card game. In the meanwhile, they passed the time by making fun of Jasper. He wasn't allowed on the steps. He squatted in the dirt. They'd all been drinking, but *nobody* could drink as much as Jasper, and they'd kept passing the bottle to him though he'd contributed not a penny to the purchase price.

224

"Yes," said Sam Dickman, "Jasper talks a good game. But he's all talk."

"That's what I been tryin' t'tell you men," said Dave Cook. "Jasper ain't nothin' but talk. It's jest like that nigger what he's always talkin' about that got away. They all get away from Jasper."

Everybody laughed.

"That's right. He ain't never killed a nigger."

"Liars! Liars!" Jasper shouted as he struggled to get to his feet. He failed and fell over on his side.

The step-sitters erupted into gales of laughter.

Tears welled up in Jasper's eyes. I'll show the bastards.

*

He found out how to locate the boy. If he hung around the path to the still, staying out of sight near where the path came out of the woods, he was bound to see the boy at least once a day. The nigger couldn't stay away from the ripe wench for even twenty-four hours. That was the boy's weakness, and Jasper was going to find a way to use it.

225

# 57

Ernest lay in the grass beside Betty Lou. He was glad she was asleep. He could not get enough of looking at her. When she was awake, he felt self-conscious staring at her all the time. He wanted to, but he didn't let himself. It almost killed him not to let his eyes spend all the time they wanted devouring her. He used all of his will to prevent them from staying on her, roaming over her. When she was asleep, he didn't have to discipline himself. He gave his eyes free rein. She was so beautiful. Smooth, deep, golden-brown skin. Rounded nose, and full, sweet lips. Curled black eyelashes. Soft, black hair with tints of brown in it. A neck like the Bible said - made of pomegranates. Her arms were luxuriously rounded. If he got at just the right angle, he could see down her blouse far enough to glimpse the tops of her full, jutting breasts. He could not see her nipples, but he remembered how they grew and swelled to his touch. Her titties were softer than anything in the world. The way she was lying, the bottom of her blouse covered her waist so it was invisible. But he knew it, how tiny it was and how her hips flared from it, dramatically, to both sides and in the back, wonderfully deep and rounded. He could see her luscious calves. He wanted to touch them, but he did not. He was afraid of awakening her. He was determined to continue feasting his eyes. He could not resist brushing her cheek with his lips. She slept so deeply he felt it would not disturb her. Nor did it.

*All my life I want to be with you,* he told her with his mind. *All my life.*

# 58

Brady and Wentworth were determined to make it plain to Jasper that he couldn't be part of the group that would stage the ambush.

He would not hear of it. Who had started all this? Whose hard work found the boy? Who was the one who had kept after it all this time? He would not stand for it. This was all his doing and he would be right in the middle of it.

"Calm down, Jasper," said Brady. "You *will* be right in the middle of it. Once we've got him, we'll bring him over t' the shed in the back of Wentworth's like we told you, ain't that right, Teddy?"

"Sho' is," said Theodore Wentworth. "You'll be the main one to question him. And then - then - for the main thing, the one we's really after - you'll be there from the start. Jest like you said - 'right in the middle of it.'"

Jasper would have none of it. Spittle flew as he raged. "What is wrong with you fools! Cain't you see? I am the key, I am the cog, I am the lynchpin in this whole thing! You cain't do it without me!"

"Jasper, Jasper," said Wentworth. "Listen to me. You can see for yourself. You ain't stable. What if you should have one o' your fits while we're waitin' in ambush?"

"Yeah," interrupted Brady. "What if you was to fall out like you done so many times?"

"That's a real possibility," said Wentworth, "a real

possibility. And we got t` look out for it. The other thing - there's no way for you to know this - and it's hard to tell you to your face - but I've got to, or you might jeopardize the whole plan. Jasper ... you smells right ripe. That boy's likely to get a whiff of you before he gets to us, and take off."

"Well, I ain't never! I ain't never heard of such foolishness in my whole life. I been the one trackin` this nigga for months - and he ain't run away from me yet!"

"Trackin' and ambush is two different things," said Wentworth. "You can track from a distance. But you cain't do no ambush from a distance. You got t` be where you can jump right out on him. So close he ain't got no where to run."

"So close he can smell you," broke in Brady. "And the trouble with you, Jasper, he can smell you when you ain't close at all."

"Has you ever noticed," said Wentworth, "don't nobody ask you t` go huntin` with them? Even when there's a bunch a good ol` boys agoin`. And there's a reason for that."

Brady chuckled.

Jasper was furious.

Wentworth bore down. "I want to make this very clear. We don't want nothin` t` mess this up. We's lucky to get this second chance. And we is determined not t` let it git by us. 'Three strikes and you out.' We don't intend to strike out.

"We all know we wouldn't never have got to this point without what you done. We's grateful. We recognize what you done. But in this little thing - you cain't be there, and you won't be there. You gon` have your fair chance with this little nigga, and when we get to his big brother. After all, he's the main prize. And I'm sure you'll leave with a little souvenir. But for

228

now, and I ain't gon` say no more about it. You ain't goin` with us tonight, Jasper Hanks."

Jasper was apoplectic with fury. But he knew what he was going to do about it. He was going immediately to get himself a bottle of hootch and he was going to drink it right down to the bottom. He'd teach the bastards.

*

Eight men hid at various points along the first quarter mile to Jack Maples' still, four of them at the capture point. The night was dark, only the slimmest edge of the devil moon hung distant in the black sky. All the men were hunters. They knew how to wait for game, still and quiet.

Once Ernest hit the trail he was oblivious to everything except following it to the still. He had done it so often, he could almost follow it blindfolded. He might as well have been blindfolded, because the only thing that filled his mind and his mind's eye were visions of Betty Lou, visions that made him crazy.

They had him down and hog-tied before he knew anything had hit him. Further along the trail, in his hiding place, Tootie didn't hear a sound.

*

Jasper was delirious with joy. He believed he had never been so happy in his life. He took another swig of white lightning from the jug the men had been kind enough to provide. He looked at the nigger tied up and thrown down on his stomach. The nigger had to rise up his head to speak, or roll over a little to the side. He looked scared to death. He should be.

"What you scared about, nigger," said Jasper. "*You* ain't got nothin` t` be scared of. Nope. You got no reason to be scared at-all. It's that little, black Betty Lou what should be scared."

He cackled. "She should be real scared. It's nine of us. And we all wants a big helpin` o` that. And if you don't tell us what we wants t` know - each and every one of us is gon` get some. I know for sure I is!" He chortled with glee.

He took another swig.

"But you - you ain't got nothin` to worry about. Because if you tells us what we want to know, we gon` set you free. And if you don't tells us, we still gon` set you free. But then - then - he, he, he, he - before we let's you go, we gon` let you watch a little show - us and Betty Lou - all nine of us and Betty Lou."

Jasper threw his head back and brayed like a mule.

Brady bent over and looked into Ernest's eyes. "All we want to know is where we can find that nigger what drives for the Northrups - alone, and in the dark."

Jasper was laughing so loud when he took the next swallow of white lightning he almost choked on it.

They didn't beat or cut Ernest. They didn't lay their hands on him at all. They just talked. They described Betty Lou - all of her parts - and what it was going to be like when they got their hands on her.

Ernest loved his oldest brother, had patterned his life after him - from the inside out - loved him more than he loved anybody in the world - except Betty Lou. He could not - would not - betray his brother. But if he didn't, he knew the foul men would do exactly what they had described. Especially that one - the worst one, the lowest one, the most disgusting one. They called him Jasper. He drooled every time he mentioned Betty. He wanted to get her on the ground, naked beneath his greasy, stinking self.

Ernest shouted as if someone had whipped him. It was a loud, incomprehensible scream, but his mind was repeating, *Stephen, Stephen, Stephen!*

*If only they said they would kill me. If only they said they would kill me. I would die. I would die to save my brother's life.* But that is not what they had said. Not at all. They had described what they would do in graphic detail. *And I - I would still be alive. I - I would have to live on.*

"Please kill me," wailed Ernest.

Jasper hooted, "You'd love that, you'd love that, wouldn't you? But I'd much rather - we'd much rather - taste that sweet meat than break yo` scraggly neck!"

Saliva poured out of his mouth as he spoke. He lapped at it with his tongue.

Ernest closed his eyes. *I'm Stephen. I'm Stephen inside. What would Stephen do? What if this was Ruth-Ann, and Stephen had to decide whether to give me up, or to give her up? I must do what my brother would do. What would he do?*

Ernest screamed and sobbed as he told them what they wanted to know. They were true to their word. They let him go without leaving a mark on him.

And the eagle was dragged down out of the sky.

231

# 59

When Ruth-Ann woke up in the middle of the night to breast feed Wynfried, she was surprised that Stephen wasn't home. She lit the kerosine lamp and looked around the room. He hadn't been there. She didn't know exactly what time it was, but she could tell it was in the middle of the night. Stephen was usually home by then, not always because sometimes something would come up late and he'd have to drive Mr. Northrup somewhere. That was more likely to happen in Massachusetts than in Florida, but every now and then it happened in Jacksonville. As Ruth-Ann breast-fed her infant daughter, she was reassured by her baby's hunger and the peaceful expressions on the faces of the other two as they slept.

At dawn, when Stephen still had not come home, she began to worry. She made sure the children were sleeping soundly, then quickly dressed and went out to find Tims and Solders.

They had not seen Stephen. Tims left immediately to go down the trail to see if the Northrup limousine was there. Solders went to look for Ernest, who was likely to be the last one in, after spending as much of the night as he could with Betty Lou Maples.

It didn't take long for the two men to find out that neither the automobile nor Ernest was anywhere on the Wenders property. They knew they were going to have to tell their father.

Mama Ona would have to wait. They were not ready for her to bring the sky crashing down on them.

Papa hitched up two mules, and with Tims and Solders sitting next to him on the wagon seat, he headed into town.

Ruth-Ann stood on the bare ground in front of the house. No one else was awake. She couldn't move. She didn't let herself think about *why* Stephen hadn't come home. She had to take care of the children. She knew that. She had to take care of the children.

*Oh, my God, how can I? Where's my Stephen gone? How can I?*

They found the Northrup limousine parked near the trailhead that led to Maples' still. It was all locked up. Nothing seemed disturbed. Stephen wasn't there. Ernest wasn't there.

*

Mama Ona's keening could be heard a half mile down the track from the Wenders house. Naomi came up from Jacksonville to be with her. The keening went on for days. There was no consoling her, but being present was important. The younger women rotated taking care of the children, except when Ruth-Ann breast-fed Wynfried.

Ruth-Ann couldn't let herself think that Stephen would never return. *He'll be back. He'll be back,* she kept telling herself. She told his sisters he probably went some place to hide. Those men - those men who'd tried to lynch him before. Maybe they were after him. But he'd get away. He had to. Hadn't he declared that he'd escape all that the South was out to do to him, to both of them and their children? Hadn't he told her with his

233

own sweet voice we are going to rescue our little family from all of that? He'd be back when it was safe.

Everyone wanted to believe that, but where was Ernest? Had they gone off together to hide? Besides, where was safer to hide than their own place? The woods. The swamps. Tattler was not the only big, fierce dog roaming their land, and all the Wenders - men and women - were deadly shots. Not even a fool or even a pack of fools would try to come in to drag a Wenders off their own property.

"Nobody's found a body! Nobody's even found a body! How can we give up? How can we give up and we don't know he's dead," Ruth-Ann kept proclaiming. She said everybody knew that Tims and Solders were the best trackers in Duval County and neither they nor anyone else had found a body. There was hope. There was more than hope. There was no *evidence* that anything had happened to the two men.

*

After a week, a hand-carried letter arrived at the Wenders house. The man who brought it said he'd been paid by some stranger to bring it, with directions on how to find the place. The letter was from Ernest. He just wanted to let everyone know that he was alive. He could never come back, he said. He was too ashamed of what he had done to his big brother, his idol, the one man he loved most in all the world. "What I have done cannot be forgiven," he wrote, "will not be forgiven, even by the Lord, God Almighty. Our Stephen is dead. I am not worthy of your love, and I cannot face you for my shame, and the destruction I

234

have brought to our beloved family."

Papa Wenders stood, then, as the rock that kept the family from disintegrating. He was deeply shaken. *I believed*, he confided to his two oldest remaining sons, *that I had built us a Gilead. Now, I know I was wrong.* But he faced his failure. Stared it dead in the eye, and did not buckle. He knew he had to stand firmly on his own two feet so that his family would have something to hold onto. For the time being, Mama Ona was not up to it. That would come later, but it would have to be in the future, a future obscured by the sky falling and crashing to the earth.

# 60

Ruth-Ann asked the Northrups if they wanted her to stay on as cook. They said they understood perfectly if she thought she had to stay in Jacksonville with her children, but if she wanted to keep the job, it was hers. She did think she needed to stay with her children, but Stephen's disappearance had sealed one thing for her. She and her children could not live in the South. One way or another she was going to have to find some way to get them out, and for the time being the Northrups were her only ticket. Until then, she knew the children would be safe in the fortress that was the Wenders family. Not even the craziest white man would try to broach it. But the family's protective reach could not extend beyond their own private sanctuary.

She remembered Calter and the strips of his skin hung on fences. She remembered that old man, coming to take her on the road, frothing at the mouth, reeking of filth - with the right, every right in the world, to take her, and claim her as his own. Though her husband was a man among men, peerless in the world - yet the monster had come, head on, reaching for her, a demented derelict who could claim her and take her as his due.

*That first day in the market. I lost ... my heart.*

236

She could not live - and her children could not live - in the land of their birth, her birth, his birth. He'd sworn they would never spend their whole lives there. She would keep his pledge. Their son, their daughters - Stephen's children - could not live in a hell of such lush beauty. A green wonder of leaves, and sky, ocean and vast inland waterways, a marvel of birds and flora, brilliant colors, the sweep of wings. With its flies, spiders, mosquitoes, biting, sucking, and hopping vermin of every description, its venomous snakes and voracious alligators. She would deprive them of such a legacy. The north with all of its miseries was surely no paradise. But it was not a utopia whose beauty concealed charnel pits of the devil's own get.

No. She would give her children, including the last child Stephen would ever father, growing in her womb, what he had bequeathed.

Hope.

*I will see to it. I'm a little bit of leather, but I am well put-together. I will provide a birth right for our children.*

*Hope.*

\*

The train ride north was lonely, and it was in the jim-crow, but it was carrying her where she needed to go, and one day, it would carry her children there, too.

237

## About the Author

David Covin is Professor *Emeritus* of Government and Pan African Studies at Sacramento State University. He and his wife, Judy, an R.N., have two daughters, Wendy and Holly; and three grandchildren: Nicola, William, and Claire. They live in Sacramento, California.